Mixtape

Simon Castles

Mixtape

Stories and essays about the 1980s

Mixtape: Stories and essays about the 1980s
ISBN 978 1 76109 513 9
Copyright © text Simon Castles 2023
Cover image: Adobe Stock

First published 2023 by
GINNINDERRA PRESS
PO Box 3461 Port Adelaide 5015
www.ginninderrapress.com.au

Contents

Introduction

One Christmas when I was a teenager, my guitar teacher and I gave each other mixtapes. This was a common thing for friends to do in the 1980s, the cassette having become – on the back of the invention of the Sony Walkman and the falling price of boomboxes – the most popular way to listen to and share music.

Cassettes didn't sound as good as the vinyl that preceded them, nor the compact disc that came after and ended the cassette's brief moment in the sun. But what the cassette lacked in auditory quality it made up for in a democratic essence. A blank cassette was cheap, back-pocket portable and – after some careful curation at the stereo, or poised over the radio, hitting the record button when a favourite song came on – made to be shared with others. It encouraged a do-it-yourself attitude to music love.

The mixtape my guitar teacher gave me has stayed in my memory for a very specific reason, and that was his decision to follow 'Panama' by Van Halen with 'The Music of the Night' from the musical *Phantom of the Opera*. Whatever you think of these two pieces of music, it is doubtful anyone had paired them together like this before, or indeed since. Andrew Lloyd Webber just doesn't usually follow the guitar heroics of Eddie Van Halen.

But therein lies the magic of the mixtape. They could be or do anything its creator wanted. They were deeply idiosyncratic, and this was true not only in the song selection but in how the card in the cassette case was designed and how the track listing was written out.

As Nick Hornby wrote in the ultimate mixtape novel *High Fidelity*, 'To me, making a tape is like writing a letter – there's a lot of erasing and rethinking and starting again, and I wanted it to be a good one.'

Anyone who has made a mixtape wanted it to be a good one. Indeed, they wanted it to be the best one ever. The mixtape was like a letter, but it was also of course like a personal soundtrack. You wanted the songs, and the order of the songs, to say something about you; to express something about how you felt – about the world, life, hopes, dreams and love – that maybe you didn't quite have the words for. You wanted the song choices to somehow express your feelings for you.

This book is called *Mixtape* because it is a mixture of things, many of them revolving around music. It contains memoir pieces, essays and short stories. Some pieces are long and some are short. There is fact as well as fiction. But the common thread running through them is that they are all, in one way or another, about the '80s, the last decade before the arrival of personal computers, the internet, emails, mobile phones and text messages.

Like a good mixtape, I hope this book says something real and true about that time.

Part 1

Memoir

Toto recall

The school choir I was in was broken up by Toto. It began when our choir came under the control of a new teacher, Miss Norman.

Miss Norman was an elfin dynamo in heels, a wearer of a deep red lipstick that would spot and smear across her front teeth when she became excited. She had a new teacher's enthusiasm combined with a shakiness of voice and manner that suggested she'd ridden the express to breakdown station before, and was ready to hop on again.

Before Miss Norman's arrival, the choir – all boys, like the school – had primarily sung about God and school spirit. But Miss Norman wanted to shake things up, to make the choir more relevant to the times (the times being the '80s, though I think Miss Norman would have been happy if we just appeared to exist after the invention of television).

She introduced to the repertoire a doo-wop version of 'Blue Moon' and then a Billy Joel song called 'The Longest Time'. It went well, too. Excited not to be singing about Jesus, we belted out Billy Joel at presentation night as if he was the baddest thing to ever happen to popular music.

The success made Miss Norman giddy – but giddy in a way you knew was a mistake. You hated to see enthusiasm like that at my school, you really did. Crushing enthusiasm was kind of what the school did best. The Latin on the school emblem may have said something about it.

Anyway, Miss Norman decided our next song would be her 'absolute favourite song in the world'.

That song was 'Africa' by Toto. Miss Norman wanted us to hear the song. She pulled the cassette out of her bag and, with a kind of ceremony, slipped it into the music room's boombox. You could see she had played the tape a lot – it was worn and crusty, and stained, as if with wine and tears.

She played the song several times through. She kept her eyes closed throughout and swayed gently, a smile playing on her lips that strained to something like resignation as the song swelled and dipped. At the line about it taking a lot to drag me away from you, it was as if she was no longer in the room, but somewhere else – a place where drums echoed in the night and men were men.

When she opened her eyes, and saw only us, a bunch of oily, stinky fifteen-year-olds, it must have been crushing. But she handed out the sheet music anyway, stepped to the piano and counted us in.

It's a curious song, 'Africa', which is off Toto's fourth album, *Toto IV*. The opening verse features drums in the night (because that's what happens in Africa), whispers, a woman on a 12.30 flight, and an old man who the narrator goes to for wisdom or melody. It also features a line about wings being lit by the moon and reflecting the stars that are a guide to some kind of redemption. So much going on there. So magic them wings. But it was the second verse that caused the problem, and in particular the line about Kilimanjaro rising like Olympus above the Serengeti.

It was my mate Frawls who pointed out the problem. Frawls, unlike the rest of us, understood music and timing and performance. On an average day, he could be heard wandering the school corridors singing snatches of Britten's *War Requiem* to himself, happy as Larry.

The rest of us had precious little talent (precious little here being a generous substitute for no). We were accepted into the choir for one reason, and that was a willingness, in a school full of thick-necked rugby players, to stand up and sing Billy Joel a cappella.

'The line about the mountain has too many syllables in it,' Frawls said after we had stumbled through the song once. 'It doesn't fit the music. There aren't enough beats for the words.'

Miss Norman looked at Frawls as if he'd said Jesus Christ was a dick-wad, and told him he couldn't be more wrong. She immediately raised her hand and counted us in again. One, two, three, four…

But we believed Frawls – and the more so as the afternoon wore on and we repeatedly failed to sing the line successfully.

We would always start the line confidently, but then find there wasn't space or time for the Serengeti at the end – and how the hell could there be when the line already included the words Olympus and Kilimanjaro?

Sometimes, we would rush the line's early words in the hope that this somehow put time in the bank for the latter ones. Other times, we would reach the final word with great assurance, punch out the first syllable, and then realise we were out of time and sort of dribble the rest. Mostly, we just shot out the line – fast, blank and unemotional.

But not once – in a good thirty attempts – did we sing the line well. Not once did the song sound remotely like what Miss Norman must have imagined in her head when she decided the choir would sing Toto, and bring her inner and outer life into some kind of beautiful harmony.

To this day when I hear 'Africa' on the radio, I marvel at the way singer David Paich manages the line, even as I continue to believe Frawls was right in saying the line has too many syllables in it for the music.

But mostly when I hear the song, I think of Miss Norman. I think of her pained expression as we massacred her favourite song in the world over and over again. I think of how her hands shook as she pressed them to her temples. I think of how the choir broke up not long afterwards, and how Miss Norman left the school.

And I think how it would be good if Miss Norman later found a choir to sing her song. A choir that knew it must – somehow – do what was right, sure as Kilimanjaro rises like Olympus above the Serengeti.

The road behind

The mythology of the classic road trip, the Kerouac kind of thing, is all about the road ahead. But when I think of road trips, I think of the earliest ones I took, which were all about the road behind. Particularly the gravel road behind.

My family had a grey Volvo station wagon. There were seven of us. Mum and Dad were up front, Dad the driver, Mum the provider of sharp intakes of breath to indicate danger. Mum also gave out the Minties, one each about every five hundred kilometres. We chewed them as slowly as possible and then sniffed and gnawed at the wrappers for extra sustenance.

My three elder siblings were in the centre row of seats. Which just left me and my twin sister Jane. We were in the car's third row, in seats that faced backwards. Our seats were black vinyl and hotter under the sun than anything under the sun. Lava times infinity, as Jane put it.

The rear-facing seat was introduced by Volvo for design and safety reasons and – my hunch – because the Swedish thought it would be funny to make the world's children carsick. Well, joke's on you, Volvo: I had only one Mintie in my stomach, and there was no way I was giving it up.

Every Christmas in the '70s and into the '80s, my family drove from Canberra to Lakes Entrance in eastern Victoria. We took the Monaro Highway, which runs north–south between the coast and the Great Dividing Range. The trip, Mum assures me today, took six to seven hours. Oh, Mum and her silly 'real time' ideas. It was a journey of at least two days.

The road between Canberra and Cooma was okay, and from Cooma to Bombala it was tolerable, even as the countryside became wilder and the death wish of the marsupials more keen. But things got rough south of Bombala. The word 'highway' is generous for what the Monaro was back then. The road was gravel for about fifty kilometres, and trees were known to lie across it, presumably having died of boredom.

Most of the trip, the windows were all down. This was air conditioning. I didn't have a window, so I could only look with envy as those in window seats were blasted with refreshing hot wind and exhaust fumes. How lucky they were to have their faces made rubbery and numb by the thunder of rushing air. To have their lips rearranged and their eyelids turned inside out. Oh, to be whipped and strangled by my own hair.

With the windows down, it was impossible to hear anything. We would shout at Mum to turn up the stereo, but our words were blown away, out over the baking plains, baffling wallabies. When the message did somehow finally make it to the front of the car, Mum would lean in towards the stereo, against the wind, and at least appear to turn the knob in the right direction. And we would go from hearing nothing, to hearing nothing.

Once we hit the unsealed road, the windows had to go up. Bits of rock and gravel pinged against the car and, had the windows been down, would surely have taken out my twin, who had a way of attracting flying objects to her head. The car was quickly coated in dirt and dust, which made it virtually invisible to the many logging trucks that were busy carrying away the forest.

As we slowly roasted, I would stare out the caked and crusted rear window at the dust swirling into clouds off the tyres. I found it impossible to anticipate bends in the road ahead because I saw only the bends in the road behind. My head and stomach swayed in the wrong direction. I breathed still and stale air, also known as my brothers' farts. It was around this point my Mintie would most seriously consider ejecting itself.

The car rattled and shuddered over the gravel. Voices vibrated, taking on the staccato rhythm of the car's failing suspension. I would hear-

Dad speaking, his voice bouncing up and down on one syllable, struggling to bounce onto the next. What is he saying? Something about stopping in Cann River for a milkshake is my guess. For if milkshakes hadn't been invented, and Dad hadn't had the promise of one down the road, he would never have set out on this trip in the first place. He might not even have risked having a family.

We'd reach Cann River hours or possibly days later. We'd peel ourselves off our seats, leaving a layer or two of seared skin behind, our screams of agony hidden beneath our cries of freedom. Then we were out on the street. I'd be happy to be out of the car, but more than that I'd be happy to be simply facing in the same direction as the rest of the family. And that direction was towards the milk bar, where beyond a doorway of colourful plastic strips to keep out flies, there were milkshakes waiting.

Round and round

Our ideas and feelings about public transport are, like most things, formed young. The early trips and experiences forever set the parameters of hope and expectation. A bus to Bondi. A tram rattling toward St Kilda and Luna Park's big mouth. The first time we catch a train with our mates and no parents.

My feelings about public transport are mostly shaped by Canberra's bus network, called ACTION, and particularly a night service it ran in the 1980s.

The last bus from the city left at 11.51. You had to be on it. Civic, the quaint name given to Canberra's city centre, was an isolated, strangely threatening place in 1987. Taxis were rare, and no teenager could afford them anyway. At 11.46, I'd stop whatever I was doing – hot chocolate at the Pancake Parlour – and run.

The late bus had two drivers, and who the driver was made a difference to how the night ended. Some nights it was a bloke we called Sunshine Sam, and, later, just Sunshine. Sunshine was, I guess, being paid to drive the late bus, but you got the sense he would have turned up either way. You even wondered if the bus was his, and on Saturday nights he simply took it for a spin and picked up a few of the lost and lonely along the way.

Sunshine could not stop smiling – maybe he'd tried it once and realised it wasn't for him. He loved Bananarama, and kept a 'best of' in the tape deck. Maybe it was stuck there. The later it was, the louder he played it – 'Shy Boy', 'Cruel Summer', 'Venus'. You really haven't experienced the nation's capital until you've been driven past its buildings and monuments to a song about a goddess on a mountaintop.

The late bus was what was called an area service. It didn't follow the usual route, but went in the direction of an area and then incorporated three routes in one.

Sunshine took this as permission to drive wherever the hell he wanted. He treated the whole of Canberra as an area to be explored. He'd get on a roundabout – one of Canberra's many – and go round and round, three or four times, as if giving himself time to think. Suspense would build among the dizzy passengers as to which exit he'd take. Eventually, he'd shoot the bus off its coil and into the dark night.

This was a lot of fun. A magical mystery tour soundtracked by Bananarama's fab three. And while Sunshine kept you guessing, he always delivered you, in a roundabout way, where you wanted to go. If the bus wasn't full, he'd even drop you at your door.

He'd pull up at your driveway in a forty-foot, bright orange bus, the engine labouring, the hydraulics heaving and sighing. The doors would fold open, and a shaft of light would pierce the nature strip, as the neighbourhood was given a short, sharp blast of 'Love In the First Degree'. You were home, and Sunshine disappeared with a wave.

Other nights, though, the late bus was driven by a bloke we called the Darkness. We called him the Darkness on account of him not being Sunshine. The Darkness was about three hundred years old. He wore the same thick woollen suit every day, whatever the season.

You heard the Darkness before you saw him. He chugged and wheezed and spittle flew from his face in terrifying arcs. He had a long black cigarette holder he never removed from the corner of his mouth. He smoked whole cigarettes in a single inhalation, the tip burning down like a bomb's wick in a cartoon. His face was set in eternal grimace, as if he'd been prematurely embalmed by a work experience kid in an Iron Maiden T-shirt.

For the Darkness, driving the area route meant pulling over when he felt like it, and grumbling to no one in particular that the service was ended.

'But where are we?' some poor soul would say, looking around hopelessly, seeking back-up, voice wavering on the edge of panic. 'I live miles from here.'

The Darkness would disappear into a cloud of smoke, and emerge right as the spit started to fly from his grizzled face. 'This is the last stop. Get out.' The cigarette holder would never leave his mouth.

It's been more than thirty years since I've seen Sunshine and the Darkness. But those trips weren't a bad introduction to a life of public transport use. Every journey I've taken since – the thousands upon thousands, away from home and back, in Canberra, Sydney and Melbourne – has fallen within the bounds of what I already knew. That a ride from here to there can be an unexpected joy, or scary as crap.

Cream and punishment

Desire helped me quickly remember the milk order for one house. But standing on the running board of a small truck that rattled and shuddered its way through the suburbs, the day's heat still rising from the bitumen, I felt sure I would never remember what all the other houses were meant to get.

I became a milkman the summer I was fifteen. So I was actually a milk boy. But who's ever heard of a milk boy? Of course if you're under thirty-five, you've probably hardly heard of a milkman either, except maybe in movies or old British sitcoms. It's a job that suggests the olden days, another time, a black-and-white world even if I did it in an '80s exploding in neon orange and pink. Being a milkman was my first job and it was disappearing even as I did it.

My first days on the job were done with another runner. He told me what milk to leave on which doorstep and to memorise it fast. The milk came in reusable glass bottles with foil tops that were red, blue or gold depending on the creaminess and fat content.

'People really crack the shits if they get the wrong milk,' my trainer said over his shoulder as we headed back to the truck, our shadows long and thin in the falling sun. 'Then the boss cracks it at us.'

My trainer said a lot as we ran along, mostly in a kind of shorthand, pointing here and there – 'Two red, one gold, four blue, one red, two gold' – but just one order stuck in my head. Three gold-top went to a neat red-brick house on a big corner block that was apparently home to a girl so pretty she had been on the cover of *Dolly* magazine.

The existence of this girl I soon learnt was common knowledge among all the boys on the milk run, who spoke in breathless tones about how she sometimes sat out the front of her house in blue jeans and an INXS singlet, listening to her Walkman, and how her frizzy hair, except for it being brown not red, made her a dead ringer for Nicole Kidman in *BMX Bandits*.

For weeks, I didn't remember any milk order but hers, and what other houses got was a crapshoot. I just tossed any old dairy product on doorsteps and hoped for the best. Was I stupid, I wondered, that I couldn't memorise the deliveries like everyone else? Was I easily distracted like my teachers said? Would I always be like this in jobs?

But as the months passed – and as the neighbourhood residents no doubt grew used to getting the wrong milk each night – a few other orders began sticking in my head. I hadn't seen the *Dolly* cover girl, but it was as if the aura surrounding her house permeated outwards, creating a kind of force field of associations that helped with recall. A house that looked like hers: two blue-top. The place three before hers: three gold-top. The home with a hedge as frizzy as I imagined her Nicole-Kidman-in-*BMX-Bandits* hair to be: one red-top.

One day, the boss told us that the local magpies had developed a taste for milk, which they got by smacking their beaks through the foil tops. He said the birds particularly went for the gold-top because it had a thick layer of cream. We were told to warn all the gold-top customers of the risk to their milk if it stayed out on the front step too long.

And so I approached the house of the *Dolly* cover girl. It was a still evening, in that after-dinner hour which is summer's magical hour, crickets chirping in all directions, and the house was bathed in a soft golden light. I rang the doorbell, looked down at my scrawny arms and quickly bicep-curled the milk crate in my hand. It didn't help. I waited for what seemed like forever and realised I had forgotten to breathe.

No one was home. I left a note under their milk, scared off a lurking magpie and headed back out into the street. The rest of the street's orders came to me as easy as a cooling breeze. Two red, four blue, one gold…

Highly strung

When I tried to learn guitar as a teenager, my teacher gave me one of those mnemonics popular in music to help remember the strings. It went: Eddie Ate Dynamite, Good Bye Eddie, and indicated the strings, from top to bottom, E A D G B E.

'But isn't goodbye one word?' I said.

'Shut up,' my teacher explained.

I nodded and repeated the saying quietly to myself as I picked out the strings one by one.

Months later, maybe a year, I scrawled a new mnemonic for the strings in my school diary. It went, Existential Angst Dread Grabs Bloody Everything. I know, catchy right? But why was I thinking this? What had changed since those carefree days when, guitar in hand, I had imagined Eddie having his guts ripped apart by high explosive?

In a word, anxiety. Playing the guitar, I had come to realise, made me incredibly anxious. Any kind of performance – and I use the term loosely to mean playing in front of anyone (even in front of myself in the mirror) – was a kind of terror for me. My heart would race. My hands would shake. Sweat would prickle my skin as if I'd been pierced simultaneously by a thousand tiny pins.

The worst experience was at a guitar summer school. I had my first ever panic attack while attempting to play 'My Bonnie' to a room of about twenty (and yes, a panic attack in the middle of 'My Bonnie' is as funny as it sounds – to see if not to experience). I remember everyone's eyes on me, and desperately wishing the other students, who sat silently with their nylon-string Yamahas, would make some noise and save me.

By eighteen, I'd pretty much given up guitar. It wasn't just the anxiety. I was a very ordinary guitarist – so ordinary the word guitarist seems wrong, like a category error. But I can't deny that a desire to escape anxiety, to run from it, was a major reason for putting the guitar down.

You can't run from anxiety, though, as anyone who has had anxiety knows. Anxiety finds you. It creeps into life under the cover of darkness, in the very shape of darkness, and makes itself at home. It becomes a weight in the chest – invisible to the eye, but there, undeniably there – and presses on the heart and lungs. I may have stopped playing guitar – employing that age-old strategy of the anxiety sufferer: avoidance – but anxiety tracked me down all the same.

So eventually I did what I had to do. I saw a doctor. I got drugs. I meditated. I learnt cognitive behavioural therapy. I found a shrink. I took up yoga. I read a pile of self-help books with terribly designed covers.

And the years passed. Decades in fact. Time in which I carried my guitar from one home to another. I didn't play the thing; I just put it in the corner of rooms. This is the fate of most of the world's guitars. To sit unplayed, the wood fading, the strings rusting. And yet I couldn't help but feel that my guitar – its sound hole like an eye – was looking at me from its spot in the corner, silently taunting me for being gutless.

Then one day several years ago, I picked my guitar up. I can't remember why I did this, but it's possible I intended to strangle it for years of torment. But for whatever reason I strummed a chord instead. This chord sounded terrible – like the opposite of the chord David played that pleased the Lord in the Leonard Cohen song. This was a chord that would have displeased the Lord immensely.

And yet, playing that terrible chord felt oddly calming. Almost meditative, particularly as I got a strum going. I was surprised to find I liked the feeling of my fingers up against the frets, the plectrum in my hand, the curve of the guitar's body on my knee.

And who cared how it sounded? Okay, my neighbours cared how

it sounded. But hadn't I learnt that one of the cures for anxiety is to care less what others think?

Now I put the guitar in my hands most days, even for just fifteen minutes. I strum like it's a mantra. Some days, I even play for my girl-friend, and she – an accomplished musician – encourages me even as I hit bung notes with what I can only call a kind of dexterity.

Recently, I came up with a new mnemonic for remembering the strings. Every Anxiety Does Get Better Eventually. And I'm hoping this one will stick.

Dogs love soft rock

When I was young, my family had a dog, Owen, who we decided had terrible taste in music. Actually, terrible doesn't quite describe it right. It was more that Owen, we believed, cared not a bit for what was hip, cool or alternative.

Owen's prime dog years were the early '90s, but Owen – a golden retriever with a lazy eye – had no time for grunge or hip-hop or indie bands. Why listen to Nirvana or Public Enemy or the Replacements, reckoned Owen, when you could tune in to an easy-listening station playing the best power ballads of the '80s?

I can't remember how it started, this belief Owen was a music dog. But we all ascribe human attributes to our pets. And at some point one of my siblings put a list up on the fridge headed 'Owen's favourite bands', and the list grew. Mr Mister. Whitesnake. REO Speedwagon. Richard Marx. Starship.

As far as we were concerned, Owen was never happier than when Foreigner's 'I Want to Know What Love Is' was emanating from the kitchen radio as he gnawed on a bone.

It turns out we may have been onto something with our hunch about Owen's music tastes. Researchers from the University of Glasgow published a study that found dogs prefer soft rock and reggae to other musical genres. To put this another way – a way the scientists didn't exactly – dogs relaxed more when listening to Toto.

'Overall, the response to different genres was mixed, highlighting the possibility that, like humans, our canine friends have their own individual music preferences,' said researcher Neil Evans, a professor of integrative physiology. 'That being said, reggae music and soft rock showed the highest positive changes in behaviour.'

It's hard not to smile at the thought of dogs chilling to reggae. As the study put it, dogs spent 'significantly more time lying and significantly less time standing' when listening to this music. Yep, nice kicking back, Fido. Bob Marley approves.

But that dogs like soft rock rings truer to me, and not just because I lived with Owen during the years he dug Air Supply.

Soft rock doesn't pretend to be cool. Soft rock feels things super intensely. Soft rock isn't afraid of showy displays of emotion. What music could be better suited to an animal that completely loses it every time it sees you? An animal that loves you so much it can barely handle the emotion of you going to the toilet and closing the door for like one minute.

REO Speedwagon sings that he's going to keep on loving you because it's the only thing he wants to do. Dogs understand this feeling.

Price check on love

In the summer of 1986, at the supermarket where I worked as a shelf-stacker, there was a girl named Emily Bottle who never asked for a price check on anything. That's why I got sacked. Well, kind of. But I'm getting ahead of myself.

On registers one and two and four to seven, the girls would ding the bells they had by their hands and shout for a price check, their appeals echoing up the aisles like a siren song. But on register three, Emily Bottle just went about her job, cool as the bubblegum bubbles she blew when she was bored.

This was in the days before self-service and barcode scanners, which existed beyond the horizon of the imaginable. Those on checkouts had to ring up everything on the cash registers manually. But first they had to find a sticky price label on every item – a label that may have become unstuck and restuck itself to practically anything in the universe. At the end of shifts, I'd find price labels all over the heels of my shoes. I once found one behind my ear. Another time, I noticed my cat was a red spot special at $2.99.

The division of labour at the supermarket was set – as set as the concrete outside the door that stretched with parked cars and shopping trolleys to a shimmery mirage: the girls did checkouts and the boys collected trolleys, stacked shelves and checked prices. It was a demarcation that gave the place the slightly charged feel of a year eight disco, with girls on one side, talking and laughing among themselves, and boys on the other, staring and struck dumb in mystery and confusion.

It was in this atmosphere that the price check became important, for it provided the only opportunity for interaction. 'The big tin of John West salmon is $4.49,' we'd report back to one of the girls, hoping it might somehow spark a conversation. 'Expensive, huh… We're living in a material world, I guess… So do you like Madonna?'

Emily Bottle had arrived in late November, put on for the Christmas rush. She had aqua eyes beneath a serious brow, strawberry-blonde hair she wore in a ponytail at the top of her head, and honey-brown arms that jangled with bangles in every colour of the '80s. I adored her with the intensity of the Australian sun. An egg cracked on my intensity would have fried in seconds.

'The new girl on register three never asks for a price check ever,' I said to my mate Rocky one day, as we priced and stacked tinned tomatoes in aisle six.

Rocky's real name was Mario, but everyone called him Rocky because his arms and nose looked like Rocky Balboa's and because he liked to punch meat in the deli. Rocky looked across to where Emily Bottle was bagging a jumbo pack of toilet rolls. A sunbeam caught one of her bangles and sent reflected light darting into our eyes and dancing up the walls and across the ceiling. Rocky looked back at me and smiled his big Italian smile – a smile that said my comment had given away too much, that my quiet teenage desperation was not quiet any more, and in fact was so loud it was competing with the store's stereo, which had just begun playing 'I Want To Know What Love Is' by Foreigner. Rocky held his pricing gun to my head and pulled the trigger.

But as the summer wore on, and the sweat beneath our shirts became stickier, and the days more languid and sluggish, Emily Bottle's silence began to bother Rocky as well. Was she, we wondered, just making the prices up? Or was it possible, improbable though it seemed, that she was yet to come across an item without a price on it?

It was while thinking on these questions that Rocky had an idea. He suggested that we not put a price on every fifth item we stacked. That we increase the number of items in circulation without a price and thus make it more likely – inevitable, surely – that Emily Bottle would have to request a price check.

'Let's smoke her out,' Rocky said finally, pleased with himself like he was a member of the A-Team.

I am not by nature an irresponsible person. In fact, most people who know me would say I'm reliable, cautious and risk-averse to the point of being if not boring then at least among boring's close circle of friends. But I can be tempted into stupidity in two ways: by a desire to please those I consider superior to me (Rocky's arm muscles alone put him in that category), and by a borderline-pathetic wish to attract the notice of spunks. (Did I mention Emily Bottle's strawberry-blonde hair? And how she wore it in a ponytail at the top of her head so her hair fell down evenly in all directions like a water fountain?)

All of which is by way of explaining why I not only agreed to Rocky's plan, but a few days later, when there had been no change on register three, when Emily had shown no sign of ringing her bell for a price check, I suggested that rather than leave every fifth item without a price, we make it every fourth.

Every fourth item quickly became every third. Then the other shelf-stackers joined in. They did this less out of interest in the original motivation (that is, Emily Bottle) than the allure of rebellion and a simple wish to be part of things. They liked the idea of trying to outdo each other in the arena of the stupid. By the last week of 1986, only about half the items that went on the shelves had a price on them. And things had officially got out of hand.

The breakdown of order at the supermarket happened like bankruptcy did for that character in Hemingway, which is to say gradually and then suddenly. First, there were a few more bells ringing than usual. Then there was nothing but bells. They rang continuously. And me and Rocky knew, even without having read Hemingway, for whom the bells tolled.

We were soon so busy doing price checks, running back and forth to the girls on checkout, that we weren't stocking shelves at all. Our pricing guns lay discarded, like rifles dropped by retreating French soldiers. There were more and more calls for price checks, which led to delays at the registers, which led to queues forming down the aisles.

Shoppers complained to anyone who'd listen – usually me and Rocky as we raced past – and those who weren't complaining had that sad resigned look like you see in '80s news footage of what supermarkets were like behind the Iron Curtain.

All this I had created out of my longing and desperation for Emily Bottle.

But love is no defence, I found, or at least it isn't according to spotty floor managers of suburban supermarkets. I was sacked. Someone had to pay for what had gone on, and it was me. I defended Rocky, and his job was spared. He took his anger out at my dismissal the only way he could – by punching meat in the deli.

I later got a job as a theatre usher, which I liked better anyway. And I like to think I left the supermarket a more social place. Who knows what young love budded or blossomed on those busy summer days when shelf-stacker boys and checkout girls intermingled intensely over the price of tinned tomatoes, toothpaste and toilet rolls?

You're wondering, though, about Emily Bottle. Well, she continued just as before. She never asked for a price check on anything, even when practically nothing in the store had a price.

But on the day I was sacked, a funny thing happened. As I walked through the supermarket for the last time, I looked across to register three. I was some distance away, but I could see Emily blowing cherry-coloured bubbles. She raised her arm, as if she was about to wave me goodbye, and then her hand dropped suddenly. And right as it did so, a bell rang. Was it her bell? Or a bell on another register? I'll never know. Could be she was just whacking a fly.

The house next door

The rat scurrying along the top of the fence convinced me it was okay to do what we did. I swear that rat even looked at me and winked, as if throwing down a challenge. I looked at the rat and thought even a rat must get stupid in heat like this.

It was the first weeks of a new year, early '90s. The temperature had been stuck in the thirties for days – long enough that you couldn't say when it started because night and day had blurred. Time had twisted like the sheet on the bed. The air was so still you could hear a hiss, almost below awareness, as if the concrete and bitumen were trying to exhale.

I had moved to Melbourne six months before. I was unemployed, as was my girlfriend Cristyn, an actor with long dark hair and a dreamy outlook the unemployment office was trying to knock out of her one form at a time. Unemployment was ten per cent – double if you were under twenty-five. We were the bastard kids of a recession.

With no job and no money to do anything, we were home a lot. Home was a run-down terrace in the inner north. We'd apply for the jobs we could, and then our days would be free, but when you're unemployed, you learn freedom has a price tag.

We had been getting on each other's nerves. Cristyn thought I was pessimistic and lacked a big dream. I thought she was careless with money. Why with rent due would you pay $35 for a video of *The Umbrellas of Cherbourg*?

And for both of us, always, there was the strain and frustration of unemployment. Each job we didn't get, each call not returned, each application that disappeared into the void, increased our isolation and deepened our disconnection from the everyday. It was us against the world, and the world didn't know we existed. The world had lost our resumés, couldn't place our names, said don't call us, we'll call you.

Our focus became the house next door. It was a house done in the old Italian-Australian style – red-brick, solid, closed off. We had never seen anyone go in or out, and a bloke up the street told us it had been that way for years.

But the house wasn't empty. Through a narrow gap in the curtains of the front window, you could make out a chair and something dark against a wall, a painting or mirror.

'We should take a closer look at that place,' Cristyn said one afternoon, and her eyes sparked with a rascal-light that had killed me since the day we met. The idea quickly gathered momentum, fell into the slipstream of the rising temperature, until taking a closer look felt inevitable.

And then I saw the rat. The rat came from the neighbour's side, and I wondered how many more rats were over there. Maybe the rat was from a colony that existed metres from where we slept each night. Maybe it was dying of thirst and on a recce before an invasion.

The rat made me think we had a right to explore the house next door on the grounds of health, hygiene and self-defence – or so I imagined explaining it to the police if it came to that.

So we found some rat traps and cheese chunks, climbed the fence and dropped into the neighbour's cement yard. We were barefoot, had been for days, long enough we had forgotten we were. Now we remembered. We hopped about on the sun-blasted cement like baby birds trying to fly. The only shade was by the back of the house. We ran there fast, on the edges of scorched feet, swearing with each step like it helped.

The yard had a raised vegie patch that had been burnt hard and dry, and wooden stakes were ridden into the ground like headstones. Towards the back fence a tin shed stood at a curious angle, as if it were slowly melting into the cement. Cristyn put her face to a window at the back of the house and cupped her eyes.

There was something about the back door that made it look unlocked, or like it had never been locked and was from an Australia of another time – a time when there was easy trust between neighbours and pavlova enough for everyone. I reached out and pushed at the door, and it opened. Cristyn looked at me and said we probably shouldn't, but I was already stepping into the house.

'Property is theft,' I said over my shoulder, not sounding convinced. 'Didn't we learn that at uni?'

It was dark inside after the sunshine, and my eyes took time to adjust. My vision swirled with stars. I breathed in deeply. The air was close and musty. Cristyn came in behind me and put a hand on my back. The sweat made our clothes cling to us like a second skin.

We were in a kitchen. It was an ordinary kitchen. It could have had someone in it yesterday, were it not for a thick layer of dust that coated every surface. It was like a still life. Pots and pans were in cupboards. A row of bakelite canisters sat on a shelf beside a stack of *Women's Weekly* cookbooks. There were dishes in a drying tray, and a tea towel folded in half over the edge of the sink.

'I think the dishes are dry,' Cristyn said.

I walked over to a calendar on the wall. It was from a local car mechanics. It showed a man standing next to a hotted-up Holden, big smile on his face, giving the thumbs up. It was a 1987 calendar and it was opened at November. On the third Saturday of the month, someone had written the words 'Gina's party' and circled them in red.

Cristyn went into the next room, but came back quickly.

'You find a body?' I said, not sure if I was joking.

Cristyn said it was a lounge room and there were family photos on the wall, and it was wrong what we were doing. She sat down at the kitchen table and lay both arms out flat, as if reaching for something. Then she put her head down on her right arm. I set a rat trap under the sink and another one on the bench by the toaster. Then I sat down as well. It was too hot to move anywhere straight away.

'Shit, what time is it?' Cristyn said, lifting her head. 'I have to get my dole form in by five.'

I didn't know what time it was. In this house, it was 1987, and had been for years. We sat in silence, as if listening – as if we might hear answers to the questions that swirled about us in the still air. Then we started talking, and words came in a rush.

What had happened here? Why had life stopped so suddenly? And if the answer was death – and death seemed the most likely answer – why had the house been left like this for years, as if waiting for someone's return? Had the whole family died at once?

We talked about whether the house would stay like this forever, even as our lives changed and we got jobs and money and moved away.

We talked about all the stuff you gather over a life, and how the stuff kind of takes over and then outlives you. We talked about our fears that you could just disappear one day, and how life would go on as if you were never there.

We talked about 1987, and how we were both at school when life in this house had ended. Cristyn remembered how that year she was in a production of *Guys and Dolls*, and how something about the show made her feel like anything was possible. She couldn't wait for school to end and life to start, but now she wondered if that wasn't life after all.

We talked on in that way for hours until the sun set, and a gentle breeze came through the door, the first stirrings of a cool change. We went home and watched *The Umbrellas of Cherbourg*.

Cristyn didn't get her dole form in. We would pay for that tomorrow. But that afternoon, it hadn't seemed like the most important thing. For a few hours, we'd needed to escape ourselves and whatever life was right then. So as the sun beat down on suburbia, we had let ourselves sink into the lives of others and the other lives of us.

Part 2

Essays

Minutes to midnight

In 1984, the Doomsday Clock kept by the Bulletin of the Atomic Scientists was moved to three minutes to midnight, its most dire position since the invention of the hydrogen bomb. Midnight Oil released *Red Sails in the Sunset* the same year, an album whose cover shows Sydney after a nuclear strike. And though I can't be sure exactly, I feel it was these two events that had much to do with a third I recall from around that time: me, aged about fourteen, sitting down to write a letter to my girlfriend telling her the end of the world was near.

As a teenager, I spent a lot of time staring at that Oils album cover. It shows the harbour dry and scarred with craters, the bridge mangled and destroyed near where Luna Park should be, downtown Sydney desolate and falling away to desert. The image is by Japanese artist Tsunehisa Kimura, but I could never see it as art. To me, it was a postcard sent from the near future. From a place without a postcard, to steal the title of another Oils album. I'd stare at it and imagine nuclear holocaust as the Oils played on my tinny oversized tape deck and formed an ominous soundtrack to homework I wasn't doing. And Peter Garrett sang about how the summer of another year brought a little more to fear.

Midnight Oil were massive in the 1980s and to young Australians, they had an authority as awesome as Garrett's towering frame in full flight across the stage. And one thing they sang about a lot – particularly on *Red Sails* and the album that preceded it, *10, 9, 8, 7, 6,5, 4, 3, 2, 1* – was the terrible unease of living during a particularly hot phase of the Cold War. A line from 'US Forces' referred to living in the shadow of the bomb – and this song on an album whose very title was a countdown to some terrible moment. The Oils never gave any false hope or comfort that the great south land might be spared in a nuclear war either. Our support for the US meant that when the superpowers began exchanging warheads, we were toast, metaphorically and literally. It would be, to quote another Oils album, species deceases.

And the feeling at that time, at least among many young people, was it could all happen at any moment. 'I look at the clock on the wall,' went one Oils song. 'It says three minutes to midnight.' I had never heard of the Doomsday Clock until I got into the Oils, but soon all clocks, if their hands were close together and pointing roughly north, made me think of the end of days. Which made me want to listen to Midnight Oil. For like great bands have always done, the Oils provided a solace by reflecting my own angst.

What seems obvious to me now but didn't then is that my fear of nuclear war and my love of Midnight Oil were bound together. The one fanned and reinforced the other. The Oils were a salve to fears they helped provoke; and I dug them for it as they filled me with more terror. It was a perfect arrangement for feeling intense all the time, which is of course an unspoken aspiration of teenagers everywhere.

But I must have been feeling particularly intense around the time I planned to write a letter to my girlfriend Amy. The penning her a letter part wasn't out of the ordinary, though I realise that now sounds ludicrously old-fashioned, as if I was dipping a quill into an inkwell. It wasn't like that, but nor was it like now exactly. The past is a foreign country, they do things differently there – which is another way of saying there was once a time without mobiles or email.

Back then a page torn from the middle of an exercise book and a well-chewed Bic pen were important communication tools. Particularly if you were at an all-boys Catholic school and your girlfriend was at the Catholic girls school across the road and you didn't see her much on account of parents who put limits on those things, for reasons you could only put down to them having forgotten, or worse never known, what love was. So me and Amy scrawled each other letters, which passed between us – sometimes with the help of intermediaries – when school broke for the day.

The letters were much the same in content – school sucks, sad I can't see you today, miss you heaps – but their similarity never stopped me reading each one I received about a thousand times. I studied them as if they were the rarest parchments ever discovered by man. Whole worlds opened up in the curl of a g, a dot above an i, something scribbled out and started again. Her handwriting was a kind of magic – its finest trick the conjuring in me of great longing.

The letters were always signed off with love and a string of kisses. Which was sweet and no doubt an expression of real feelings – well mine at any rate. I was smitten. If it wasn't love, it was, for me, the first flood of worship, which is an awful lot like love, only with more pimples and blushing and bad hair.

But there was something slightly out of place about me filling my letters to Amy with all the love and kisses I could fit onto a scrap of exercise book paper. For I had at that point done nothing more than hold her hand, and I had hardly even done that. I hadn't had a 'pash', which to me was just a wonderful word for some kind of wonderful I knew nothing about. As for sex, well, it happened in another universe from where I sat chewing the end of my pen.

So my letters had an element of play-acting about them. I was much more passionate on paper than in person. Face to face, I had too many other things to think and worry about, beginning with how to occupy my limbs and when was a good time to breathe. Only safely away from Amy's presence would my nerves calm enough to allow me to express anything I was actually thinking or feeling.

Which explains the letters in general, and the letter I wanted to write in particular. For what I wanted to say in this one I could never, ever have said to her face. It was this: if the world comes to the brink, if we hear it's minutes to midnight and the bombs are about to fly, if Ronald Reagan moves to usher in the Armageddon he clearly believes in and perhaps secretly longs for, well, if all that happens, could we maybe get intimate in a way we haven't, which is to say any way at all? Could we, or you know, um, should we, get closer before a Russian intercontinental ballistic missile lands in our vicinity and we only have time to mutter 'holy shit' before our eyeballs melt and run down our cheeks?

Yep. That is what I imagined I would say, or something like it anyway. Of course, were I to write such a letter, I would follow in the steps of countless million boys and men before me who have used any pretext imaginable to try to get into a girl's pants. But I don't think that occurred to me at the time, or perhaps I just like to believe it didn't. What I did know was that I planned to make the letter so full of hedging and equivocation and qualification that the central point would almost be lost on the page. That I hoped would both allow the question to be asked, but also give me plenty of wriggle room if Amy reacted negatively or with complete bafflement.

'Oh that,' I would say, if she suggested I was suggesting what I was indeed suggesting. 'I was just joking around. You know how thinking about Reagan and the largest nuclear weapons build-up in history always puts me in a silly mood.'

Which it did. But also in an impending doom kind of mood. A long, creeping shadow of death kind of mood. A mood that was captured in lines that jumped out at me from Midnight Oil songs I played over and over. Lines about bombs in a row, missile stockpiles growing, the final hour and ashes flying in the wind.

In the latter half of Midnight Oil's career, when they enjoyed their greatest international success, the band's songs revolved mostly around issues of land rights, corporate greed, the environment and even love and spirituality. For that reason, it's easy to forget just how apocalyptic the tenor of their work was in the early '80s. In retrospect, it's not surprising that the Oils featured in several scenes of John Duigan's 1984 film *One Night Stand,* which was about four Sydney teenagers who hear that nuclear war has broken out in the northern hemisphere and together face what might be their last night on earth. I felt an instant connection with the characters in the film for the simple reason that they, like me, had Midnight Oil as the background noise to their fears about the end.

But while the Oils were the dominant background noise for me in this respect, there was other music in the mix. Other songs on the soundtrack to my worries about the world. How could there not be? In the '80s, there was a stack of pop songs about the bomb – at least if you were listening out for them. To name just a handful of tracks on a list that ran long, as if to a mushroom cloud on the horizon: 'Breathing' by Kate Bush (1980), '1999' by Prince (1982), 'Seconds' by U2 (1983), '99 Luftballoons' by Nena (1983), 'Walking in Your Footsteps' by The Police (1983), 'Two Minute Warning' by Depeche Mode (1983), 'Forever Young' by Alphaville and then 'Laura Branigan' (1984/85), 'Two Tribes' by Frankie Goes to Hollywood (1984), 'Russians' by Sting (1985), 'Guns in the Sky' by INXS (1987) and 'Everyday is Like Sunday' by Morrissey (1988).

There was also a Smiths song that, while mostly about Morrissey's deep feelings of inadequacy (and what Smiths songs weren't?), included a line that summed up my thoughts at the time almost perfectly. Morrissey sang about how if love didn't bring a couple together, then the bomb surely would.

The Frankie Goes to Hollywood track was the biggest hit, pushed to the top of the charts with the help of an entertaining film clip that showed caricatures of Ronald Reagan and the Soviet premier Konstantin Chernenko fighting in a ring, with the United Nations a crazed audience cheering the madness on. It was the Cold War as world championship wrestling. The video ends with the earth exploding. Asked about the song years later, the band's frontman, Holly Johnson, said, 'There was paranoia in the air. There was the uncomfortable feeling that it could all happen at any time.'

What made Midnight Oil stand out for me from these other acts was the uncomfortable feeling they gave that it could all happen at any time right here. By bringing the fear closer to home, they made it more real. The Oils were Oz rock, and to Oz kids in the '70s and '80s, that was important in a way that is hard to explain and almost impossible to overstate. Oz rock signified a rough integrity, a ballsy honesty, an us-versus-them ('them' being an umbrella term that covered, among other things, soft rock, techno music, pop acts that were posed and pseudo, users of too much hair mousse, and, in some overarching sense, those cultural imperialist invaders America and Britain). Oz rock meant a sound that was guitar-heavy and genuine, and an energy and attitude that couldn't be manufactured because it had its roots in a thousand sweaty and beer-soaked gigs in pubs across the land.

Midnight Oil showed fans a country they recognised, even if they didn't always want to see. In their songs was the Australia of red dirt, blue sky and dry creek beds, but also the Australia of sunbaked suburbia, the bus to Bondi and McDonald's franchises from here to the horizon. In their songs too was a country dangerously on the skid from casual and comfortable to acquiescent and apathetic. As novelist Tim Winton said about the Oils, 'The music contained an unmistakable atmosphere of the suburban Australian life I was part of. Underneath the bland, safe surface, a jerky agitation, an itch I recognised… Australia seemed about to stop thinking and just go shopping and here was a band anxious about our communal future.'

So great in fact was Midnight Oil's dismay at where things were heading that they even flirted with calling it quits for the greater good. In 1984, just as *Red Sails* was hitting record shops, the band threw its support behind Peter Garrett in his run for the Senate as a Nuclear Disarmament Party candidate. Had he won, that would probably have been the end for the Oils. But he lost, and I remember being secretly happy about it. Much as I wanted a world without bombs, I also wanted Midnight Oil to never die.

But I could understand Garrett and the band's sense of urgency. I felt it too, and I contributed to the global call for action by worrying more than ever before. By 1984, the superpowers were essentially behaving like teenagers after a falling out, and weren't talking to each other. A *Time* magazine cover had an illustration of Ronald Reagan and Yuri Andropov with their backs to each other, both looking as icy as death. Inside was a warning that the leaders 'share the power to decide whether there will be any future at all'.

The future seemed to hinge on the success of deterrence strategy, also known as Mutual Assured Destruction (or MAD). This was the theory that one power would not launch a strike against another for knowing that a bunch of bombs would shortly rain down on their heads in return. But even as a teenager, I could see the flaw: there was no real way of being sure it worked until a nuclear exchange demonstrated that it didn't. It relied, moreover, on the leaders of the world being rational and sane. And where was the evidence for that? To me, the Soviets seemed scary and crazy for all that wasn't knowable about them; the Americans for all that was.

My memory of the Soviet leadership in the early '80s was of a man who appeared dead, and soon was, being replaced by a man who looked like the man who appeared dead and soon croaked as well, only to be succeeded by a man who looked like the man who looked like the man who appeared dead, and so on. None of it inspired great confidence that the world would exist much longer than the latest decrepit Soviet leader.

The Reagan administration meanwhile put the fear of God into everyone, which I think was party platform. In 1980, the year he was elected president, Ronald Reagan told an interviewer that 'we may be the generation that sees Armageddon'. He then set about making this the goal of his first term. He called the Soviet Union an 'evil empire' and committed his country to the development of a space-based nuclear weapons defence system that became known as Star Wars. It all seemed about as connected to reality as a game of Space Invaders.

I found the blurring of the distinction between the real world and the world of computer games and movies terrifying. That a nuclear exchange might be started by accident because of some breakdown in what was fact and what fiction seemed entirely plausible to me. I had seen *WarGames*, the 1983 film in which a game-playing computer geek almost triggers nuclear Armageddon through misadventure. At the time, it didn't seem that far-fetched. For teenagers of the '80s, just as for the president, what was on the screen could easily be real and perhaps was. Annihilation was just a red button on a joystick away.

Martin Amis has written that 'your feelings about nuclear weapons depend among other things on your date of birth'. And certainly for the youth of the '80s, the bomb was a unifying fear, in the way terrorism or climate change is for the young today. It's probably also true more generally that the threat of nuclear war transfixes certain types more than others – with the young and the anxious (and maybe Midnight Oil fans) at or near the top of the list.

I have no recollection, for instance, of my parents or any of my teachers being concerned. Did they, to steal the subtitle of *Dr Strangelove*, learn to stop worrying and love the bomb? As Einstein wrote in *The Menace of Mass Destruction*, 'Most people go on living their everyday life: half frightened, half indifferent, they behold the ghostly tragicomedy that is being performed on the international stage…'

Age probably has something to do with reaching this state of half indifference. As people get older, a really big childhood fear can lose its grip, partly because it has been faced for so long that it grows acceptable, even comfortable, through familiarity, and partly because a thousand other fears crowd it out. The boy who expressed his dread of the bomb in the 1950s with the words 'Please, Mother, can't we go some place where there isn't any sky?' presumably grew up to accept living under it wherever he was.

Adults also lose a lot of the creative and imaginative power they had as children. They don't do as much of the 'what ifs?' and 'what happens next?' that spark the imagination but can also be at the core of worry and anxiety. The adult thinks 'Don't go there', but the child is already there, looking around in wonder and alarm. As the US Institute of Medicine put it in their 1986 publication *The Medical Implications of Nuclear War*, 'To contemplate the threat of nuclear war requires an act of the imagination which is difficult, if not impossible, for most adults. It requires young people to venture into an unknown and uncertain territory, into which many of the adults around them will not travel.'

Talking to friends, I wasn't surprised to hear many of them had as teenagers ventured into this unknown and uncertain territory. What was surprising was to hear about the thinking and planning they did in response. As their parents went about day-to-day affairs, seemingly unconcerned, they were considering the practicalities of protection and survival. Where is the best place in the house for a fallout shelter? How can a door and boxes be used to make a lean-to inside a bunker? Which materials create the best barrier against radiation? Which windows should be sealed and painted white to reflect the heat? How much water and tinned food is needed to make it through a nuclear winter, after toxic clouds of dust and smoke block out the sun?

I didn't think about such practical stuff much myself. Surviving a blast seemed too unreal to me; being a goner too certain. Martin Amis remembers how his teacher instructed students to use the desk lid to protect themselves from a nuclear attack. 'I sensed violence and absurdity that lay beyond contemplation,' he writes, 'and I expelled it from my conscious mind.' I think I felt something similar, even if I couldn't have put it into words.

What was in my conscious mind, however, as I contemplated nuclear war, was my letter to Amy. For a period that was probably only weeks but which in my memory feels longer, as if it encompassed at least a term of the Reagan presidency, the idea of writing the letter bounced about my brain. It absorbed my waking hours, which came to include many of the dark and silent ones before dawn. The other things in my life – school, footy training, homework, telly, pimples – went on as semi-usual; I attended to them, but only with what can best be described as steadfast inattentiveness. I was preoccupied. In my head was a bigger picture and it had Amy in the foreground and a mushroom cloud ripping up the horizon.

This had to end, of course, and it did. It ended the day I stopped wrestling with the idea of writing the letter and instead sat down to actually write it, whereupon I quickly found I could not. And I couldn't because I had no words, and words are required for the composition of a letter. Even with Midnight Oil playing on the stereo, ramping up the intensity, pressing home the urgency of now, inspiring me to action, nothing came from my pen. Words escaped me, as if words too had taken refuge from a threat. My attempts at getting the letter down repeatedly foundered, usually after the 'Dear Amy' part, which however strong an opening couldn't make up for the lack of, well, the lack of anything below it.

So why did I have such trouble writing the letter when I had thought about it so much? Why the block when I had written it in my head a thousand times? Why had I stalled when the superpowers still had forty thousand warheads ready to fly at any moment?

Sitting at my desk, nervously tapping my pen along to drummer Rob Hirst's pounding rhythm, I found I wasn't able to put what was in my head onto the blank page without hitting a snag. And the snag, ironically enough, was fear. More fear. This was fear not of nuclear war, but of everything related to the idea of writing and sending the letter. The fear of embarrassment. Of ridicule. Of bringing attention on myself. The fear of uncertainty and change. Of judgement and punishment. The fear of guilt and shame.

And what if I did actually manage to write and deliver the letter, and got the reply I wanted, or imagined I wanted? What then? The more I thought about it, the more I realised that not only did I fear Amy would reject my sexual advance, but also that she might not. In fact – as my pen hovered shakily over the empty page – it struck me with some surprise that the latter scared me considerably more.

I was, you may recall, a Catholic. I had even been an altar boy. And that is a problem when your mind is on the cutest girl in school. For the thing about a Catholic upbringing is that it tends to make you believe that whatever you're thinking or doing, or thinking of doing, is most likely wrong or bad in some way. Which of course makes thoughts about attraction and sex completely fraught, and opens up whole new avenues of fear as adulthood nears.

So I come to a central point here, though it might more aptly be called a punchline (Catholics at least being good at laughing at themselves): my fear of nuclear war was trumped by my fear of sex. Compared to physical contact with a real flesh-and-blood girl in all her wonderful mystery, nuclear cataclysm seemed not quite so scary after all. A big fear was diminished by being eclipsed.

In trying to write the letter, I had raised the spectre of adulthood, and the sight of it had sent me running in the opposite direction. Running fast too, as if from an atomic blast. All at once, I wanted to remain a child for as long as possible; to back away from life's epicentre until it sucked me in. And if nuclear war broke out in the meantime, and a bomb was dropped on my city, well…so it goes. It wasn't like I would be around to rue the things I didn't do. In a flash of blinding light and heat too intense to imagine, I'd be ashes in the wind, if that. Time would stand still and I'd be forever young. Amy would be too. The thought was almost comforting. So I scrunched up the letter and threw it in the bin.

I still find myself thinking about those things, and about that time, when I play my old Midnight Oil albums. It's as if the memories are retained in the songs themselves, and are released the moment Rob Hirst brings his drumstick down hard on the snare. There's a secret history captured in this music: of suburban adolescence; of skinny and sunburnt Aussie teenagers, in singlets and flannies, full of restless energy and anger and dismay, as the Cold War superpowers faced off one last terrifying time. Midnight Oil also rocked. To me and my schoolmates, they were a reflection of great angst, but also a wonderful release from it.

Around the time I was contemplating the letter, there was a disco at my school, and Amy was there. I don't remember much about the night, but at some point the deejay put on a Midnight Oil song and announced a competition to see who could do the best impersonation of Peter Garrett dancing. A bunch of us entered – our duty as Oils fans – but none of us got very far. None of us that is except for Amy who, despite being only half Garrett's height and having a full head of golden locks, blitzed all comers. She got Garrett perfectly, as if she'd channelled him. The jerky and jolty convulsions, the stiff and sudden electrocutions, the arms thrashing the air, the hands outstretched, the whirling like a rogue dervish.

Under a school hall disco ball, Amy danced to Midnight Oil like there was no tomorrow. I stood there and watched on in awe. I watched her spin away and then back again, the walls and floor showered with a thousand lights like stars. And for a moment I didn't have a worry in the world.

Born in the ACT

Greasy Lake sounded more fun than Canberra's Lake Burley Griffin, but it was beside the latter I was born and around its waters I grew up. The former lake features on a track from Bruce Springsteen's 1973 debut album, and can be found 'about a mile down on the dark side of route 88'. There some lost souls, including Crazy Janey, Wild Billy and Hazy Davy, get teenage-silly drunk, scrap in the mud and dance under the stars like spirits in the night. I've been to Greasy Lake many times in the thirty years I've liked Springsteen, even though it doesn't exist.

Lake Burley Griffin does exist, but it's an artificial creation, dreamed up by an American architect and backed by Sir Robert Menzies until somehow it was right there beneath his dark and wiry eyebrows. To many, the lake is emblematic of Canberra: pretty enough to look at but not quite real.

As teenagers, me and my mates swam in the dank lake, which made us feel sick, and drank sun-warmed beers on the shore, which had the same effect. Under a high and cloudless Canberra sky, we would gaze at the pontoons in the distance, and at the dead fish floating by closer in, and play music on an oversized tape deck until the batteries died and the music warped to a drawl. We listened to the Oils and Chisel – and, because I forced his music on my friends, to Bruce Springsteen.

I would daydream about Greasy Lake and the many other places in Springsteen songs – 'a rattlesnake speedway in the Utah desert', 'the beach at Stockton's Wing', 'that dusty road from Monroe to Angeline', the Trestles, 'the fields out behind the dynamo'. Places that seemed more magical, and yet paradoxically more real, than where I was. I would listen to 'Born in the USA' and wonder about being a Springsteen fan who was born in the ACT.

Everyone ruminates some on their home towns, but I suspect Springsteen fans bring an above-average intensity to these reflections. And they do this no matter where their home towns are or how different they might be to Springsteen's own birthplace – the small, working-class town of Freehold, New Jersey. So much of Springsteen's music is, after all, about origins. About where you were born and how you are stuck. About place and circumstance, and how these shape and fuel dreams of escape, even when actual escape isn't possible and it's only the dream that is in any sense real.

What Springsteen would make of a place like Canberra – of 'my hometown', to quote one of his song titles – I'll never know. But, in many ways, a less Springsteen-like place is hard to imagine. Springsteen songs seethe with the rage and desperation of working-class life, while Canberra is possibly the most comfortably middle-class city that has existed anywhere ever. Springsteen sings of factories. Canberra doesn't have factories, unless you count the warehouses in Fyshwick that mass-duplicate porn movies. Springsteen tells of Thunder Road, of streets of fire, of going racing in the street. Canberra has roundabouts and wide, mostly deserted avenues.

But Springsteen also sings about how fire is impossible without a spark, an observation that some might argue captures Canberra's problems as a city almost perfectly. The national capital may have the country's most permissive laws around fireworks, but the city is hardly seen as sparky. In the Australian imagination, Canberra is not synonymous with fun. And when I recall all the crap Canberrans cop because of this, the endless put-downs they endure, I'm struck by the thought that Springsteen's music might have an unlikely resonance for those born in the ACT after all.

Growing up in Canberra, you are forever being told your city is boring, sterile, weird, soulless and disconnected from the real Australia, the implication being that you had better get out of there if you want to know what living is. Me and my friends could hardly miss the message, and when the time came, we left, almost to a man and woman. To be born in the ACT was in some senses to be born to run.

Canberra was chosen as the site of the capital because it sat roughly midway between Sydney and Melbourne – almost as if its founding idea, its very reason for being, was proximity to elsewhere, nearness to the places that mattered. To grow up in Canberra was to feel the pull constantly of the two great Australian metropolises your city was artificially created to exist between. And the Hume Highway beckoned in both directions, offering a promise like that in Springsteen's 'Thunder Road' about how two lanes can take you anywhere.

It would be too neat to say I was playing 'Thunder Road' or 'Born to Run' when my car left the Canberra city limits and I headed for Melbourne to live twenty-five years ago. Truth is, I don't remember what was on the stereo or even if it worked. It would also be contrived to say I put pedal to the metal, since my 1982 Mazda hatchback's fail-safe response to speeds over seventy was to shake violently and break down.

But what I did know back then, even before my car headed slowly in the direction of Yass, was that in Springsteen songs the road out of town promises salvation but doesn't deliver it. Real escape is a mirage. Your problems come with you, and plenty that is vital stays behind. All that would prove true, so thanks for the heads-up, Bruce.

In the last line of 'Thunder Road', the narrator says that 'it's a town full of losers, and I'm pulling out of here to win'. This ghostly greaser swaggers with the sweet certainty of youth. But the man who wrote these lines in his early twenties now lives about a half-hour's drive from the town where he was born and which he wanted to escape from with such steely hunger. Springsteen may have been one of the tramps born to run, but in the end he didn't run far – or more accurately, he did run far, but then retraced his steps, as if looking for clues to what made him run in the first place.

Unlike Springsteen and the many lost and longing souls who populate his songs, I was never running from anything much to begin with. I was a lucky middle-class kid legging it from a small city everyone said was boring, so I could have a lucky middle-class life in a big city that apparently had it all. Hardly a song in it. Yet one of the great things about Springsteen is precisely that in his songs all lives, all stories, are imbued with a certain romance and glory, and listening to him helps you see traces of a quiet majesty in your own small tale.

As comedian Jon Stewart said when paying tribute to Springsteen, 'When you listen to Bruce's music, you aren't a loser, you are a character in an epic poem…about losers.' From that perspective, there are millions and millions of characters in Bruce's epic poem. Characters from all around the world, even the Australian Capital Territory. People running and falling back. Working on dreams and waking from them. Longing for horizons even as horizons are closing in.

After my father died, I was in Canberra more often, borne back into the past. I find I like the place more as I get older. Lake Burley Griffin might not be Greasy Lake, but time and memory have made it seem just as magical to me.

Sometimes when I drive over Commonwealth Avenue Bridge, I find myself gazing over to the spot on the lake where me and my mates used to hang out – to the sun-baked banks where we would daydream the days away and think life was happening elsewhere. And it's almost as if I can hear Springsteen's guitar floating over the water, reminding me I never ran very far.

Famine and fame

The song seemed an anomaly. Or a moral corrective in a time that needed one. In the middle of the '80s, a decade remembered for ostentation, selfishness and greed, a song called 'Do They Know It's Christmas?' was released by a pop star supergroup calling itself Band Aid. It wasn't much of a track – even its writers admitted that, while Morrissey called it 'daily torture on the people of England' – but it made an appeal to our common humanity. Think of others this Christmas.

The appeal was heard, even if the song, which was impossible to escape in the weeks before Christmas 1984, quickly began to grate. Over and over it played, on radio and (the then-booming) music television. It was like permanent background noise, part of the ether, a relentless poke at the conscience, as we in the West threw turkeys and hams and mince pies into trolleys, and children stamped their feet for Cabbage Patch Kids and Ewoks.

The song was an incredible success – at the time, the best-selling single in British chart history. The record sold faster than it could be produced, went to number one around the world, raised millions of dollars for famine relief in Ethiopia, and set in motion a movement that would lead, only months later, to Live Aid, the most famous charity concert in history.

But more than just a big hit, 'Do They Know It's Christmas?' was also, according to Bob Geldof, the crotchety Irishman behind it, a symbol of people rejecting the selfish values of the '80s. 'It was all of us saying to ourselves, "We're not that",' he said. 'We're not all wearing red braces and driving Porsches with loads of money. We're not. There are other values that this planet has and that we hold dear as individuals.'

It was an appealing idea, and perhaps partly true. In a decade in which the people of the West were encouraged – via the triumphs of Thatcherism and Reaganism – to put the self and ambition above old ideas of society and solidarity, the opportunity for a hardened populace to show a semblance of unity and compassion was probably welcome.

But if the song appeared from a certain perspective to run counter to the prevailing ideology and spirit of the time, seen another way it was perfectly in keeping with it. That's why it worked so well. The song, and the story behind it, encapsulated a lot that was true about the '80s (and the decade's legacy), including the cultural and political conservatism, the distrust of government to solve anything, the growing faith in celebrity, the depoliticisation of poverty, and the rejection of the last vestiges of '60s progressivism and '70s punk for a sharply-dressed, free-market pragmatism.

Bob Geldof was a fading rock star in 1984. His band the Boomtown Rats couldn't land a hit to save themselves, with the charts in England (and indeed America and Australia, where a second British invasion seemed under way) dominated by New Romantic acts such as Duran Duran and Spandau Ballet. Thanks to the rise of music television, the times were made for pop stars with great hair and designer threads who looked good standing next to supermodels on yachts. Bob Geldof wasn't this.

Despondent about his career, Geldof switched on the BBC news on the evening of 23 October 1984, and, in his words, 'saw something that placed my worries in ghastly new perspective'. It was a report by correspondent Michael Buerk on the famine in Ethiopia. Over harrowing images of bloated, starving children and wailing mothers, who moved wraithlike over ground of moonscape grey, Buerk described a crisis of 'biblical' proportions in a place that was 'the closest thing to hell on earth'.

Deeply shocked and moved by the report, Geldof was motivated to act. And whatever criticism there is of what followed – some justified, some not – you can't fault Geldof on the determination he showed to do something. His response to what he had seen was very human, and he turned it to superhuman energy.

Little more than four weeks after seeing the news report, Geldof had managed, with the help of friend and Ultravox frontman Midge Ure, to write a song and corral about thirty of the biggest names in English pop into a London studio to record it. The song was laid down and mixed in a manic twenty-four hours – Boy George flew in from New York by Concorde at the last moment to sing his lines – and released just two days later. The record had a sleeve by Peter Blake, the pop artist who had designed the iconic cover of the Beatles' *Sgt Pepper's Lonely Hearts Club Band.*

By Christmas '84, the single had sold three million copies in Britain alone, and would go on to sell nearly twelve million worldwide. There were stories of people buying fifty copies, and giving forty-nine of them back for the record shop to sell again. 'Everyone bought the record, even if they didn't like it,' said Geldof.

To watch the video of 'Do They Know It's Christmas?' today is to be struck, '80s cliché though it is, by the hair. So much hair everywhere, except on Phil Collins's head. And almost exclusively male hair too, since women were not well represented in Band Aid (Bananarama practically flew the female flag alone). There's Bono's mullet. Midge Ure's ponytail. George Michael's Princess Di. Sting and Paul Weller's schoolboy fop. And the Spandau boys versus the Duran boys in a battle for the best tease, curl and crest.

But once you get past the hair – and yes, this takes a while – it is the lyrics you notice. Such as Bono's famous line, delivered with typical Bono brio: 'Well, tonight thank God it's them instead of you.' Really? Is that what the songwriters wanted to say? Someone's going to starve, so thank Christ it's not me? Similarly clumsy is the Christmas toast line, as we're asked to raise our glasses to 'them, underneath that burning sun'. Somehow cheers doesn't feel quite right, does it?

Michael Buerk, whose news report had been the catalyst for the song, summed up the feelings of many when he said, 'It's a nice enough song, but complete bollocks actually.' He also made the point that Ethiopia had a different calendar to the West, so to be wondering in song if Ethiopians knew it was Christmas was a bit daft since for them it wasn't.

More troubling, though, was the way the song perpetuated us-and-them myths about Africa. 'Where nothing ever grows / No rain or rivers flow' went another line. No rivers flow? Not even the Niger, Nile and Congo? By placing the blame for poverty and famine purely on natural causes, on false ideas of Africa as the unlucky continent, the song removed politics – where much of the culpability did actually lie – completely from the picture.

It was true there had been a terrible drought across Africa's Sahel region in 1984–85, but the famine that struck Ethiopia was caused as much by war and the policies of the country's communist government as it was by geography or climate. Nature was only partly to blame for this crisis.

That the song didn't reflect any of that was hardly surprising, however. It was Geldof's firm resolve that Band Aid be non-political. He believed response to the famine was a moral issue that transcended politics. More to the point, he didn't want anything getting in the way of the song's sole objective – making money.

While Geldof's stance was understandable – leaving aside the fact that choosing to be non-political is itself of course political – it gets to the nub of why the song worked as enterprise but failed as art or protest. Why the song has so little force or power outside its historical moment (unlike, say, John Lennon's 'Happy Xmas (War is Over)', a track Geldof originally hoped his song would emulate). The Band Aid song held back. It was interested in symptom, not system. It was a cry for dollars, not change.

In the documentary *Band Aid: The Song That Rocked the World*, Bono says, 'We were like the bastard children of the Clash, who actually believed that music could change the world.' But in reality, the pop stars of Band Aid had neither the desire for real change of their '60s counterparts, nor the anger of the '70s punks to reject the system entirely.

By the middle of the '80s, pop stars were no longer a threat to the establishment; they were the establishment. They weren't railing against the system, they were part of it. The stars of Band Aid were as good a representation as existed of the growing power of celebrity culture. It was precisely that which allowed them to raise so much money so quickly.

They deserve credit, of course, for putting the growing power of celebrity to good use, even if their success doing so arguably changed the nature of charity itself. In the years after the triumph of Band Aid, charity and activism became less and less about grassroots action, and more and more about celebrity-driven spectacle. Geldof and Ure surely played a role in this shift; they helped position goodwill in the slipstream of cultural and free-market forces.

Indeed, it is interesting to note that Geldof has admitted in the years since Band Aid to having a certain admiration for the great champion of neoliberalism, Margaret Thatcher. He even called her a 'punk' because she took on every old institution she saw. And it's not hard to imagine the Iron Lady having a grudging respect for him too.

In a decade that celebrated individualism and the charismatic tycoon, Geldof was the rock star entrepreneur for charity. He was Saint Bob, cult CEO of the global good deed. In a sense, he privatised aid – and he did it right at the time government was winding back more generally on its postwar commitment to the notions of society and welfare. Geldof took up slack, in other words, as the state went into a care deficit.

Geldof and Ure and a bunch of big-haired pop stars did care and they did achieve something remarkable with Band Aid. With initial hopes of raising £72,000 for famine relief, they ended up banking £8 million (and this was before Live Aid). The money helped buy, among other things, 150 tons of high-energy biscuits, 1,335 tons of milk powder, 560 tons of cooking oil, 470 tons of sugar and 1,000 tons of grain. 'I know that our song saved lives,' Ure wrote later. 'How many songwriters can say that?'

But whether Band Aid changed anything in the longer term is of course more open to question. Getting aid to the people who needed it also proved much more difficult than those involved had expected, with Geldof in the end forced to confront what he'd tried so hard to avoid – politics. Indeed, it was politics – in particular, the need to break a truck cartel in Djibouti that was hindering the transport of aid – that was the impetus for Geldof to move on from Band Aid to staging the Live Aid concert.

Bono may have liked to think, or hope, that he and his fellow '80s pop stars were the bastard kids of punk who could change the world with a song, but the reality on the ground was tougher, the politics more intractable, the ideologies of the times more fixed. Years after 'Do They Know It's Christmas?', the U2 frontman made another observation about Band Aid which got closer to the truth about the song and its legacy. 'We have to now face facts, and realise that Band Aid was just that – a Band-Aid. What is underneath that is the gaping wound of inequality.'

Summer of when?

Even in the summer of '85, the year the song was released, it didn't make much sense that Bryan Adams was singing about the summer of '69. Check out the video. He looks so young, as if he's in a school battle of the bands comp and is just glad to be free of zits for the big day. Surely he can't be feeling that nostalgic for a youth he appears to still inhabit? And why the longing for a year in which none of the song's events could have happened?

But I'm not here to bash Bryan Adams or even the song particularly. The song is what it is – a heavily-nostalgic, sepia-toned, radio-friendly rocker about being young and all the usual stuff (music, friends, girls). It shouts out unashamedly that they are the best days of your life, and has no time for the counterclaim that memory is a liar.

Adams and long-time writing partner Jim Vallance even titled an early version of the song 'Best Days of My Life'. But at some point 'summer of '69' entered the lyrical mix, and became dominant.

It is the '69 that has always struck me as the song's false note. Even hearing the track for the first time as a fifteen-year-old, the date seemed all wrong, as if it didn't really belong and had been tacked on as an afterthought, as a way to tap into some hippie, free-love vibe that in truth Adams hadn't experienced any more than I had.

Bryan Adams was nine years old in the summer of '69. It is of course possible that he played guitar until his fingers bled before he reached double figures, but did he really have a girlfriend who told him it would last forever, and a band that fell apart because one of its members got hitched, all before he was out of the fourth grade? Maybe Prince could pull that off, but clean-cut Canadian Bryan?

Vallance has said that one of the song's influences was 'Running on

Empty' by Jackson Browne, and particularly the line 'In '69 I was 21'. But the crucial point here is that Jackson Browne was twenty-one in 1969. He was getting high and getting laid that glorious summer – he had seven women on his mind (see 'Take it Easy'), which is presumably why he was running on empty.

But for all that the song's references to '69 bother me, I feel Bryan Adams's pain. Or at least I empathise with his position.

If you were born or came of age after the '60s – particularly immediately after – it was hard to escape the feeling that you had somehow been born too late. That there had been a bang-on party, and you had missed it – that maybe you had even have killed it by showing up.

This sensation was reinforced by a thousand TV shows, movies and songs on classic rock radio that banged on about the '60s until you understood perfectly why Kurt Cobain wanted a tie-dyed shirt made with the blood of Jerry Garcia.

To grow up in the enormous freaking shadow of the baby boomers was to live with the endless mythologising of a time you never knew, but which you came to feel you knew. It was a textbook example of what Douglas Coupland calls 'legislated nostalgia' – having memories forced on you until they were kind of yours.

Woodstock happened in the summer of '69, but it was as if all of us who came after had our heads shoved into that soil in upstate New York until we smelled the glorious residue of Mary Jane and hippie arse-crack and declared it holy ground.

So I can picture Bryan Adams over his writing pad, wanting to put some words down about the summer of '76 or '77 (surely the real summers of this song), but finding his time lacking, or at least lacking in a mythology that would easily translate into a multi-platinum record.

And maybe he scrunched up a dozen pages and took three-point shots at the bin in the corner before he realised that if he just set the song in the '60s how this made things come alive, because everyone already had feelings about the '60s (not real ones but that didn't matter), and how these feelings (youth, freedom, rebellion) were just the ones he wanted his song to be about. And bam! Suddenly he's singing about the summer of '69 as if he was in bed with some flower babe in love beads when man landed on the moon.

Bryan Adams would, of course, dispute this take on the writing of his song. In fact, several years ago he came out and said that 'Summer of '69' was about, well, a sex position. 'One thing people never got,' he said, 'was the song isn't about the actual year 1969 – it's about making love à la 69.'

That's right, that song you've been humming along to as you drive the kids to soccer is actually the soundtrack to chapter nine of the *Kama Sutra*.

If what Adams says is true, then the apostrophe in the song's title is confusing, a fig leaf (or perhaps suggestive of a 69 involving a mysterious third object). But co-writer Jim Vallance, for one, rejects any seamier take on the song, saying that while writing it 'at no point did we discuss implied meanings or references'. He recalls Adams's main influence being the super sweet and innocent 1971 film *Summer of '42*.

I suspect Adams's latter-day highlighting of the sexual connotation is an attempt to give his song more edge and credibility – something it never had in abundance.

But I also like to think Adams tired of singing about the '60s – about a time that wasn't really his in the way the song made out, and which had been mythologised to the point of meaninglessness.

So Adams switched things around in his head. And now when he gets up to sing his song – when he belts it for the thousandth time – he's in the right place. Rather than thinking about a time he didn't really experience, he's remembering a sex act he probably did. And the memory is sweet enough to taste.

iPhones killed the boombox star

According to a legendary AC/DC song, 'rock and roll ain't noise pollution'. The track, from 1980, conjures a time when Chiko Roll-munching, Big M-sucking Aussie youths played bands like Acca Dacca stupidly loud whenever and wherever possible – and hoped to hurt the ears and sensibilities of the oldies along the way.

Most Australians over about forty know the AC/DC song I'm talking about, even though only a minority would actually own the album the song is on, *Back in Black*. Which kind of suggests the song's claim is untrue. Rock and roll can be noise pollution.

After all, everyone heard this track whether they wanted to or not. Even those who didn't like Acca Dacca (heretics or, in the vernacular of the times, 'poofters') had Angus Young's screeching guitar solos inflicted on them from all directions.

In Australia in the '70s and '80s, along with the noise of jackhammers in the streets, TAA planes overhead and loud mufflers on hotted-up Toranas, there were blokes and chicks who blasted music over sunbaked suburbs. Who imposed their tastes. Who shook us all night long.

But things changed a little with the arrival of the Sony Walkman, and then a lot when we entered the iPhone age. Today, playing music has become a much more private experience.

The kids who once carried boomboxes or ghetto blasters around and forced everyone to listen to whatever rocked their world are now kids with iconic white buds in their ears. The iPhone has silenced the music of the stranger in public.

There's still plenty of music in the city, of course. Buskers bang out 'Hotel California' and other classic radio hits. Shops play whatever music some research company says will put people in a buying mood.

Mobile phone ring tones offer five-second grabs of 'Sweet Child o' Mine'.

But there's less of the music of strangers bouncing off buildings. Less music played loudly and publicly by youth just cos they wanna.

In the iPhone age, everyone has their own private soundtrack as they walk the streets, which means the streets themselves no longer have a soundtrack. More music than ever is being played privately as people use iPhones to cocoon themselves against everything, but the upshot in the public sphere is a greater musical silence.

Many will welcome this development. And part of me does too. Most of us will be able to recall being somewhere – on a train, in a park, on a beach – and having a relatively tranquil experience ruined by some spotty, seething shoe-gazer's desperate need for every soul within a one-kilometre radius to hear a selection of his favourite death metal tracks. In the '80s and '90s, most adults at some point wanted to take to a boombox with a baseball bat.

But however annoying a stranger's loud music can be, now that we're in the iPhone age I sometimes find myself missing it. And I can't help thinking something valuable and life-affirming has been lost.

The iPhone is a wondrous invention, don't get me wrong. It allows us to have all the songs we love in our pocket. I want my iPhone as much as anyone ever wanted their MTV. But there is a price to pay for iPhone love – and the price is social disengagement.

We iPhone users turn on, tune in, drop out. With the white buds in our ears – a modern look that sends a clear message of 'do not disturb' – we are oddly vacant in urban spaces even as we inhabit them.

And as we walk the streets blissing out to a very private and very personalised soundtrack, shared musical experiences become more rare. The music of others is blocked out. We hear more and more of the songs of our choosing, and less and less of anyone else's.

The loss is not only the music we no longer hear, but all the acts of having music foisted upon us that we no longer experience – and what those acts mean.

When a stranger forces music on us by playing it loudly in our vicinity, their motivation might be to draw us in or to offend us, they might do it out of joy for life or in anger and rebellion at it. But the impulse is a seeking of some sort of human connection – which is exactly the opposite impulse to the one that has us reaching for our iPhones.

Were AC/DC to release 'Rock and Roll Ain't Noise Pollution' today, the song's rebel yell thesis would be sadly spot on – because except for the fans who downloaded the track to play it privately on their iPhones, who would ever hear it?

For the love of CDs

There's never been much love expressed for compact discs. Vinyl and cassettes have their fans – serious, serious fans – and the associated media boosterism. But CDs? Whoever comes to their defence or admits any kind of sentimental attachment to them?

Which could lead you to conclude that a piece of shiny polycarbonate plastic is simply unlovable, end of story. But I don't believe it. I don't believe it because I love CDs myself, but more than that, I think a more widespread love for CDs is inevitable in the years ahead (which makes my current position both avant-garde and deeply lost in the past).

I was thinking about this on a recent visit to a big-chain entertainment store after being struck by just how small the CD section had become. The space given over to vinyl, meanwhile, had expanded and pushed into CD territory. The set-up reminded me of how record shops looked in the '80s, when CDs first moved in on vinyl. It was as if the switch was on. As if time had reversed.

It hadn't. I was forty-five, not fifteen, and Whitney Houston was a symbol of fatal excess, not a bright young thing with a pastel scrunchie in her hair who just wanted to dance with somebody.

More to the point, however retro the store looked, actually everything had changed. Today, the whole idea of recorded music as a tangible item you buy in a store and hold in your hands is passing into history. Sales of vinyl may be up, but the numbers are small.

But that CDs now occupy a cultural no-man's-land and will likely be wiped out before long is nothing if not a sign that their moment to receive some love is coming. We have, after all, been here before – with those old favourites, vinyl and the cassette.

Serious music fans love vinyl because of the beauty of the objects themselves, and the warmth of the sound – the crackle and pop as the needle hits the groove. They also like the ritual of playing a record at a time when ritual in general is being lost to the convenience of a life lived in clicks and clouds.

The cassette retains a special place, meanwhile, because of its iconography and symbolism, both of which are more durable than cassettes themselves. Cassettes represent do-it-yourself, a reclaiming of the means of production, even if all you ever wanted to do with those means was impress some guy or girl with the most perfect mixtape ever.

But the truth is it wasn't until vinyl and cassettes all but disappeared in the late-'80s and '90s that love for them really took off. Obsolescence made them precious. Cultural scarcity made them cool. And nostalgia did the rest.

Wanting a copy of Neil Young's *Harvest* on vinyl or Cyndi Lauper's *She's So Unusual* on cassette wasn't simply, or even principally, about the music or a particular quality of the sound. It was a search for a lost time. And I can't believe coveting a copy of Radiohead's *OK Computer* on CD – on the format for which the album was made – won't fill a similar need in '90s kids as their youth becomes a memory.

When CDs arrived in the mid-'80s, it wasn't – at least in my memory – to widespread complaint. OK, boomers grumbled a bit about having to replace vinyl collections, and how it was a bonanza to the bank balances of Sony, Warner and the Eagles that they didn't need or strictly earn. But to anyone younger, CDs held an undeniable appeal.

CDs had a futuristic quality. Light danced across them in all the colours of the rainbow. You could throw them around and they wouldn't break or scratch (not easily anyway, and everyone gave it a red-hot go). You could skip straight to the track you wanted, or shuffle songs – revolutionary changes we now take for granted.

More than anything, CDs sounded amazing. This is a fact easy to forget if you're a certain age, and almost impossible to appreciate if you weren't alive when the cassette was the dominant medium in popular music. Cassettes were dull and clunky; they would jam, unspool and warp so that Bono sounded like the backward-speaking dwarf in *Twin Peaks*.

To go from cassettes to CDs was like stepping from black-and-white into the Land of Oz. It was as if Dire Straits had set up in your lounge room, and sunlight through a window was hitting Mark Knopfler's red Stratocaster and kaleidoscoping everything into a future more brilliant than you could imagine.

OK, this is a bit much. Nostalgia will do that to you, make you stupid and all. But the point is, as CDs vanish from the culture, we are bound to remember what we liked about them in the first place, just as we did with cassettes and vinyl. Which is to say, CDs will have their moment even as their time disappears.

Billy Joel and the tyranny of cool

With a shrinking feeling, I pass the CD to the cool muso guy behind the counter. He gives me a quick look – do I imagine it? – like he thinks I'm a bit pathetic. Like he holds me responsible for the struggles and empty pockets of every great pop artist I've never heard of – responsible even for the slow death of rock'n'roll itself. I've just become roughly the 100-millionth person to buy a Billy Joel album. And I'm paying for it in cool points.

Buying popular music, particularly if you're old enough to remember *Countdown*, often comes with the feeling that you're transgressing cool laws. But when you pick up a Billy Joel album, you don't just feel you're being uncool; you know it. The piano man is immensely popular, but few would argue that Billy Joel's what you'd call hip. More typical are dismissals of the kind offered on *Queer Eye for the Straight Guy*: Billy Joel, one of the style queers said, is 'the iceberg lettuce of rock'n'roll'.

Yeah, it's a good line. But for all that's wrong with Joel – and there are enough valid criticisms of him to fill a grand piano or two – he's more maligned than he deserves to be. Music snobs who make fun of him irritate me considerably more than Joel's worst songs ever have (and 'We Didn't Start the Fire' and 'Honesty' irritate me quite a lot). I think it's time critics gave him his due. And if I find this hard to state publicly, that's because I live, as we all do in the West, under a tyranny of sorts. That being the tyranny of coolness.

Cool is the dominant ethic in the developed world. Cool drives consumer capitalism. Gangsta rappers will even kill for cool. 'It is only a slight exaggeration,' write Dick Pountain and David Robins in *Cool Rules*, 'to say that movements in cool are reported with the same gravity that was once reserved for the gold standard.'

But despite cool's constant movements, somehow cool has always given Billy Joel a wide berth. Cool has no truck with short, funny-looking, earnest, radio-friendly, super-wealthy, baby boomer, classically trained piano players from Hicksville, Long Island.

The American pop culture writer Chuck Klosterman is an out and proud Billy Joel fan, but even he admits that the man who shot to worldwide fame in the '70s and '80s is not cool. Indeed, as Klosterman notes, Joel is rare among popular musicians in not being cool in any way – not in the conventional sense, nor in the self-destructive sense, nor in the hackneyed 'he's so daggy he's cool' sense.

'Joel is the only rock star I've ever loved who I never wanted to be (not even when he was sleeping with Christie Brinkley),' Klosterman writes. 'Billy Joel is not a larger pop construct or an expansive pop idea. Billy Joel is just a guy. And that's why – unlike someone like Jeff Buckley – his records wouldn't seem any better if he was dead.'

But just because Joel isn't cool doesn't mean he's no good. If he's struggled to win over critics, despite being in the top half-dozen top-selling pop music acts of all time, it is perhaps partly because he wanted to win them over so badly. It is not cool to look like you want something, and Joel has always come across as wanting critical respect very much indeed.

Joel was a pretty decent amateur boxer in his youth (twenty-two wins, four losses, one broken nose), and the pugilist in him has struggled to stop swinging wildly at those who won't recognise his talent. He used to read bad reviews aloud on stage and then dramatically rip them up into bits. In his song 'It's Still Rock and Roll to Me' he stroppily attacks rock critics – and girlfriends, managers, everyone – who fail to love him just the way he is.

But if Joel sometimes comes across as try-hard, a bit desperate for recognition, so too do the reviewers who want to dismiss him as talentless. Reviewers such as Robert Palmer in *The New York Times,* who said of Joel, 'He has won a huge following by making emptiness seem substantial and Holiday Inn schlock sound special.' Or Paul Nelson in

Rolling Stone: 'His material's catchy. But then, so's the flu.' Or *Village Voice* critic Robert Christgau: 'He poses as the Irving Berlin of narcissistic alienation, puffing up and condescending to the fantasies of fans who spend their lives by the stereo feeling sensitive.'

These reviews are entertaining, but what they also make very clear is that the desire to be cool isn't limited to rock stars. Music commentators are often deeply desperate to be cool. They are also often intensely bitter at not being a great musician, rich, famous and hooked up with a supermodel. Joel dated Elle Macpherson before Christie Brinkley, by the by.

Integral to coolness is non-comformity and an oppositional attitude. The cool person must be separate from, but seen by, the mainstream. It's a risky series of negotiations. For the music critic to pull coolness off, he or she must be contrary. Which explains the power play we've all seen a thousand times: the critic who heaps praise on an act when they're not popular, and then shoots them down when they are. The music press liked Joel's early albums, the ones that didn't sell. But once *The Stranger* came out in 1977 – with its singles 'Just the Way You Are' and 'Only The Good Die Young' – and the great unwashed began loving Billy Joel, the scribes lined up to kick the little man at the baby grand.

Mainstream success is by far the greatest threat to an artist's coolness there is. It's very hard to play the rebellious outsider when everyone's throwing love and money at you. The upshot of the mainstream embrace can even be lethal. Think of Kurt Cobain. The Gen-X anti-hero could never accept that Nirvana had become what he despised – a band dug by Joe Six-Pack and on high rotation on classic rock radio – so he took matters into his own hands.

Very few artists make the transition from cult status to stratospheric popularity without having cool points deducted for every dollar they earn. But as Nick Hornby once wrote about Bruce Springsteen, 'Sometimes it's hard to remember that just because a lot of people like what you do doesn't necessarily mean that what you do is of no value whatsoever. Indeed, sometimes it might even suggest the opposite.'

Of course a song like 'Piano Man' is hard to stomach now – and one can only imagine how hard it must be for Joel to play. Everyone has heard it a thousand times – on MOR radio, in department store lifts, performed by every cheesy lounge tinkler on earth, and bawled out by karaoke crooners who believe, in their sozzled state, that they are the first person to ever experience pain. This five-minute waltz of a song simply can't bear the weight of its own success. But is this Joel's fault? Can he really be held responsible for everything that has happened to 'Piano Man' since 1973?

If I try really hard, I can kind of remember hearing 'Piano Man' if not for the first time then at least the first times. It was the mid-'70s, some family road trip or other, and the song was emanating softly and scratchily from the tape-deck speakers of our grey Volvo station wagon. At the age I was – seven or eight – I certainly didn't think the song hokey or contrived. Hearing about Paul the real-estate novelist, who never had time for a wife, and Davy who was still in the navy, and probably would be for life – well, it all just seemed incredibly sad. It evoked an adult world a lot lonelier and more desperate than I knew existed.

Chuck Klosterman thinks this way Joel has of depicting loneliness is central to why he has connected with so many millions of people around the world. Joel 'musically amplifies mainstream depression,' he writes. Joel is certainly qualified for the job; he knows that of which he sings. His father walked out on the family when Billy was seven, he's had a couple of broken marriages, a long battle with alcohol, and in 1970 attempted suicide by chugging a bottle of furniture polish. 'Joel's best work,' writes Klosterman, 'always sounds like unsuccessful suicide attempts.'

But Joel delivers much more than a piano-and-voice soundtrack to everyman loneliness and depression. At his best, he blends suburban attitude and drama with Broadway theatricality and schmaltz. In an earlier age, he might have been at home in Tin Pan Alley or the Brill Building, turning out hook-heavy and perfectly crafted popular music.

It's true he's written some awful songs. And when I listen to his albums, I tend to skim and skip a lot. That a best-of Billy Joel album includes 'We Didn't Start the Fire' makes me queasy in the same way that a best-of the Beach Boys includes 'Kokomo'.

But Joel's back catalogue is large, and there are dozens of songs I like. Songs such as the anti-aspiration anthem 'Movin' Out (Anthony's Song)', with its heavy riff and heavy warning that working too hard to buy a Cadillac-ac-ac-ac might just give you a heart attack-ack-ack-ack. And the pure 'wall of sound' pop of 'Say Goodbye to Hollywood'. And the Springsteenish 'Allentown', a track Paul Keating once cited as a favourite, thus demonstrating that even an economic rationalist can get emotional over a factory closing down. And the New Wave rocker 'All for Leyna', in which for a change it's the man going bunny boiler crazy after a one-night stand. And, well, 'Uptown Girl'.

'Uptown Girl', I hear you cry! The one that had the video clip of a big-haired Christie Brinkley dancing in the garage with all the blue-collar mechanics singing into their spanners! But that's so daggy. Yeah, well, that's just maybe. But ultimately nothing is cool or uncool but thinking makes it so. We're basically all like Beavis and Butthead, slouched on the couch watching MTV and dividing music into either 'rocks' or 'sucks'. That's how cool operates – on a binary logic. In order for some things to be cool, other things must, by definition, be not cool.

Viewed from this perspective, Billy Joel has served a valuable cultural role for more than thirty years. In being the pop star who is not cool, he has allowed others much less talented than he their opportunity for coolness. And you could say that's a pretty cool thing to do. Or you might just say, give the piano man a break.

Following Fonzie over the shark

The two women next to me at the café were doing the newspaper quiz. One was reading out the questions. I was trying not to listen, but we were on one of those communal tables that make me think of mealtime at school camp.

'The term "jumping the shark" was inspired by which TV series?' the quizmaster one said.

The women, who were in their early twenties, were silent for a beat, and then burst out laughing. It was a universal laugh – the one that means, 'We're not doing well here.'

'What the hell is "jumping the shark"?' one of the women said, and they were both off laughing again.

It's hard not to join in a quiz. It may even be impossible. And I blame Tony Barber and being weaned on *Sale of the Century* in the '80s for the fact my hand was pressed on an invisible buzzer. I jumped in. 'It's *Happy Days*. The answer is *Happy Days*.'

The women looked over at me.

The quizmaster turned the paper upside down to check the answer. 'Correct!' she said.

I apologised for eavesdropping and interrupting, but then of course started telling them all keen like about the term 'jumping the shark', and how its origins lay in an episode where Fonzie literally jumps a shark.

So keen was I to share my knowledge on this subject, that something one of the women said had taken several moments to register in my mind – a mind that was, to be fair, being flooded with images of the Fonz on waterskis readying for his big jump. But what she had said was, 'I've never heard of *Happy Days*.'

I can only say it's a sobering moment when you realise not everyone knows who Fonzie is. I suddenly saw that I may as well have been talking about a character on '50s radio serial *Blue Hills* for all the sense I was making.

'Jumping the shark' refers to that moment when a TV show or cultural product ceases to be what it was – when it strays irretrievably off course. But the term is a reminder, too, of just how brief the moment is for anything to be at, or even anywhere near, the centre of things. Of how quickly things move on.

In that moment of talking about Fonzie to two women who didn't know who or what a Fonzie was, I thought that if TV shows jump the shark, then people – whose time on earth is increasingly measured out in, and mediated by, pop culture, by the TV shows, movies and songs they consume – well, they jump the shark also.

The women went back to their quiz. I returned to my coffee, and consoled myself with the thought that *Happy Days* continued for seven seasons even after Fonzie jumped the shark.

Part 3

Stories

Madonna

Shriner, Blinko and I sat on a small grassy hill across the road from the paper shop and stared at a poster of Madonna that hung outside. The poster was in a wire frame and a breeze made the whole thing rattle and flap.

'It's like she's trying to break out of it,' Shriner said, rocking from side to side like he needed to pee. He took a drink from his chocolate milk. Shriner was crazy for chocolate milk. He seemed to use it to calm himself when feelings became too much, which for Shriner was most of the time. 'It's a sign, it has to be a sign!' he went on. 'You ready, Davy?'

I felt my guts tighten. 'Why's it me again?'

Shriner and Blinko kept their eyes on Madonna, as if worried she'd disappear if they looked away.

'You wear glasses and look smart,' Shriner said, his voice catching and squeaking on the last word. 'And your voice doesn't do what mine just did. Also you look like someone who might buy a newspaper.'

'Me and Shriner look dumb as proverbial shit,' Blinko said by way of back up, his eyelids flicking up and down a quick half dozen times. He blinked a lot, which is why we called him Blinko.

I picked at the grass by my feet, tore off blades and flicked them away. I wondered why I always got the bad jobs. Like that time at school when I was pushed into putting a bra on the statue of Mary. Why was it me up there with the granny bra between my teeth, and not Shriner or Blinko or one of the other boys standing around? Still, hard not to laugh. The bra stayed on Mary for three days before a teacher came with a ladder.

We all looked back at Madonna as a sudden gust of wind made the poster frame swing away from the wall.

'She's trying to fly to us!' Shriner said. He drank his chocolate milk, tipping the carton high to get the last drops.

I stared hard at the poster, hoping it would give me courage. It was of the magazine cover but blown-up big. Madonna wore a dark suit over a black, lacy top, and a bunch of necklaces, including one that ended in a crucifix. Her lips were cherry-red and a black ribbon sat in blonde hair that was teased and slightly darker at the roots.

I thought of how angry my parents would be if I was caught stealing the magazine. I pictured the look on my mum's face. The shock and disappointment. Her making the sign of the cross and turning away. A wave of dread swept over me.

'We could just steal the poster,' I said.

Blinko sighed and shook his head. 'Davy, Davy.'

I knew what he was going to say next because in the three days since the September 1985 issue of *Playboy* had come out he had said little else.

'It is the right of every teenage boy in the world to see Madonna nude,' he said again.

Shriner nodded as he ripped open his chocolate milk carton. 'Blinko's right,' he said. He licked along the folds of the carton at a faint smudge of chocolate powder. 'I mean, they call the magazine *Playboy*, not *Playman*. And we're boys. That has to mean something.'

I was about to say it meant nothing when the wind suddenly picked up. The poster frame holding Madonna banged against the paper shop wall, three or four quick times, detached itself and flew into the air. It glided towards us a few metres, dipped and slammed to the road. It skidded along the bitumen, throwing off tiny sparks, and wedged under the wheel of an old yellow Mercedes parked at the kerb.

'Holy shit,' Shriner said, jumping up.

The torn milk carton fell from his hands and joined a swirling gust of dust and garbage.

And even I had to admit it did seem like a sign. A flying Madonna.

*

We had a plan of sorts based on something Blinko had read in a book called *The Summer of '42* about three boys trying to buy a pack of condoms. My role was to secretly slide the magazine into a newspaper and buy the newspaper. Shriner would provide distraction inside the shop. And Blinko's job was to stand out front and sing at the top of his lungs if he spotted any parent approaching while the plan was in action.

I stood now over the newspapers and pretended to consider the selection. From the corner of my eye, I could see the magazine, piled twenty or thirty high. It was glossier than other magazines. It was like there was a halo over that part of the shop. I picked up the *Financial Times* and looked over the front page. New banking regulations. Price of gold up. Reagan taking on the aviation union. I rubbed my chin as if giving the matters great thought.

Mr Horace, the shop's owner, was behind the counter, holding a price-tag gun away from his body, straining through ancient spectacles to make out a number or the place of a decimal point. He was wiry and stooped, with hair that gripped stubbornly to the sides of his head but had abandoned his dome years ago. He had worked at the paper shop for as long as anyone could remember. I wondered if he'd even know who Madonna was.

The door to the shop opened, setting off a clanging bell, and Shriner walked in. He didn't look at me. His eyes were down on his feet, and I worried a moment he was going to walk straight into a display of greeting cards. But he stepped around it and made his way to the counter, his hands going in and out of his pockets like he wasn't sure what to do with them.

'I need a pencil for art,' Shriner said to Mr Horace. 'For school. For art for school.' He shot the words out, louder than necessary and sounding somehow guilty before the fact.

'Ah yes, pencils, good,' Mr Horace said. 'Pencils, pencils.' He put down his price-tag gun, pushed his glasses to the bridge of his nose, and headed towards the back of the shop.

Shriner followed behind, catching my eye as he walked past, a grin playing at the corners of his mouth.

The pencils thing was planned. Pencils were in the back corner of the shop, far from where the magazine gave off its holy glow. And we knew Mr Horace was obsessed with pencils. Everyone knew it about Mr Horace. Our parents said he had once been an artist, and to me it was as if an interest in pencils kept him connected to the person he once was that no one really remembered except him. And now he ran a paper shop. Adult life was incredibly sad if you dwelled on it for even a second.

I moved slowly towards the magazine, holding the newspaper out in front of me as if it was hard to tear my eyes from such fascinating financial news. A Billy Joel song played on the radio. It filled the shop with sound – more sound than I ever remembered the shop having before. Would I hear Blinko above that? What if he was out there now, trying to warn me my mum was approaching, and I couldn't hear him because of Billy Joel?

I listened hard for any sound from outside, but couldn't hear anything, not even the wind. What I could hear no problem was Shriner and Mr Horace. Shriner was asking what the H stood for in an HB pencil.

'Ah, now that's an interesting thing,' Mr Horace said. 'As far back as the 1840s, in Europe –'

'And what does the B stand for?' Shriner said, interrupting and not doing great a great job of being normal.

I wished I could have given him a chocolate milk. It wouldn't have made him normal, but might have calmed him down while Mr Horace gave the history of the HB pencil, and allowed me time to do what I had to do.

I considered backing out and blaming it on Shriner and Billy Joel. But then I was standing over the magazine and Madonna was looking up at me. A fluorescent panel flickered in the shop's ceiling above my head, casting a gentle strobe lighting across the face of the magazine. It was like Madonna was at a disco. Shriner would no doubt see it as another sign. I stared at the big words that jumped out from the cover – 'Madonna nude' – and thought of how much Shriner and Blinko would like me if I got the magazine, and how angry they'd be if I didn't. I reached out a shaking hand.

The magazine was so smooth my fingers slid across the cover. I stopped, held my breath and looked over at Mr Horace. He was fully focused on Shriner and waving a pencil around excitedly like it was a conductor's baton. Sweat prickled under my arms. *Do it now, Davy, do it now.* I got a grip on the edge of the magazine and pushed it fast towards the newspaper. There was a slap and rustle of paper.

And like that, it was done. Billy Joel was still singing on the radio, Mr Horace was saying something about a particular pencil and how van Gogh was never without one, and I had the magazine inside the newspaper and the newspaper in my hand.

I turned towards the counter, thinking how well things were going, when I heard a strange sound. It started soft but quickly became loud, completely drowning out the radio. It was low-pitched and gravelly, and so tuneless it hurt my ears. There were words, but it was like they were gulped down or strangled before they had life.

The sound was coming from outside. I looked to the shop door just as it swung open and two nuns from the school, Sister Josephine and Sister Angelica, swept in as if carried by the wind. They came straight towards me – with the determined, take-no-shit stride of every nun I've ever known – and as they approached, in what seemed ridiculous fast motion, my brain finally caught up with what I was hearing. It was the warning. It was Blinko singing.

I spun to dump the newspaper, but the nuns were on me, their black shoes squeaking on the lino as they came to a fast stop. Sister Josephine was looking over her shoulder in the direction of the terrible noise, her mouth open in silent laugh and showing lots of teeth and old silver fillings. She smelled of the convent – a netherworld mix of mothballs, disinfectant and shepherd's pie.

'Your friend is singing out there, Davy Wells,' Sister Josephine said. She raised her eyebrows so high they disappeared beneath the band of her veil.

I went to reply but her hand flew up by her ear. She wanted to hear more from outside.

'Is it "Material Girl"?' she said.

I listened hard, trying to detect something that resembled melody beneath the layers of horrible sound. 'I suppose it is "Material Girl", sister,' I said.

Blinko stopped singing at that moment, at the end of what I think was a chorus, as if he'd just been waiting for someone to name the tune, or at least recognise that it was a song.

There was a sudden heavy quiet, like the way the peace after a jack-hammer powers down is deeper than any other.

'It's windy today,' I said to fill the silence.

Sister Josephine smiled and I tried to smile back. My fingers tingled with the tight grip I had on the newspaper. I could hear Shriner asking Mr Horace if HB pencils only came in grey. I nodded to Sister Angelica, who none of us had ever heard speak and who always just followed at Sister Josephine's shoulder, bowing her head and acting peaceful and generally creeping us all out.

Sister Josephine was looking around her like she'd never been in a paper shop before. She fiddled with a wooden crucifix that hung from a black ropy cord around her neck. 'Madonna,' she said. 'We're here for Madonna.'

In my panic and confusion, and with the echo of Shriner's version of 'Material Girl' still in my ears, I almost said I was too. But instead I looked down at the *Financial Times*. 'I was just getting this,' I said.

As I raised my arm, I felt the magazine slip inside the newspaper. I scrambled my hands around the edges and quickly found myself hold-ing the newspaper at an odd angle to the sisters and kind of thrusting it up at them, straight armed, and one of my knees had risen up as if to catch anything that might fall out.

Sister Josephine and Sister Angelica turned their heads to the side to see what I was holding.

'You like financial news, Davy?' Sister Josephine said, looking doubtful.

'Oh yes,' I said, slowly lowering my leg. 'The shares, love the shares. The shares and the, um…' I chased for a word from the term of commerce I did in year seven. 'The debentures.'

Sister Josephine nodded her head slowly. 'Well, Jesus said render unto Caesar the things that are Caesar's, and unto God the things that are God's,' she said. But she didn't seem entirely convinced, and after a pause she added, 'Money does terrible things in this world, Davy.'

She then did something I didn't expect. She leaned down and picked up the pile of *Playboy* magazines, every single copy, turned and placed them in Sister Angelica's upturned arms. 'Thank you, sister,' Sister Josephine said. 'Not too heavy?'

Sister Angelica shook her head, looking as serene as ever as she adjusted the magazines in her arms, letting them slide against her belly for support, never once looking at the cover.

'Yes, it is a terrible thing, money, if not used wisely,' Sister Josephine continued as she motioned Sister Angelica towards the front counter. 'Just look at the trouble it's got Madonna into, poor girl.'

I couldn't find any words in response. But, adjusting my grip on the newspaper, I followed behind, as it seemed Sister Josephine had more she wanted to say.

*

Shriner, Blinko and I stood again on the small grassy hill across the road from the paper shop. The wind had dropped now, but leaves and rubbish still spun in little circles as if an electric current ran through them.

'Where should we look at it?' Shriner said, hopping from foot to foot and tossing a pencil into the air.

He had bought a pencil in the end – a Faber-Castell 2B, a Mr Horace favourite – and I had bought the newspaper with the magazine hidden inside. Mr Horace had put the transaction through in a kind of daze after selling twenty-five copies of *Playboy* to a couple of nuns.

'What about under the house at my place?' Blinko said. 'There's a good light down there now.'

'Cool, but let's have a quick look now,' Shriner said, reaching for the newspaper in my hand. 'Just the corner of a centre page.'

I pulled the newspaper away. 'Maybe we shouldn't look at it at all,' I said, the words surprising me as they came out of my mouth.

Shriner and Blinko looked at me as if I was joking. Over their heads I could see Sister Josephine and Sister Angelica walking the long road back to the convent, carrying the magazines they would soon drop in an old incinerator in the back corner of their garden.

'What are you talking about?' Blinko said, his blinking increasing in speed and intensity. 'It's the right of every teenage boy in the world –'

'Is it a right, Blinko?' I said. 'A right like the right to clean water that we see Madonna nude? Sister Josephine just told me Madonna never wanted these photos seen. She said some photographer just sold them off for the best money he could get. Did you know that?'

Shriner threw his arms out like he could care less. 'But what about all the signs,' he said. 'Like the poster flying off the wall, Madonna flying towards us? We're totally meant to see Madonna nude.'

'You wanna know about signs, Shriner,' I said, my voice rising. 'What about the sign that at the moment I had the magazine in my hand, the very second I had the magazine, I received a visitation from two nuns from the Sisters of Mercy on a mission to save Madonna? That sure seemed like a sign.'

Shriner and Blinko looked at me, still not sure if I was joking. Then Shriner lunged for the newspaper. I was ready and lifted the newspaper above my head. But as I raised my arm, the magazine slid out the bottom and fell to the grass with a gentle slap. And then it was as if time slowed. For what felt like a long moment, Madonna stared up at us from the ground, seeming to say, 'Come here, boys,' but maybe saying, 'Back the hell off.'

I threw the newspaper at Shriner and Blinko, the pages unfolding and coming apart in a blur of black and white, and got my hand to the magazine first. I snatched it up, turned and ran. I could hear Shriner and Blinko swearing and then the sound of their footsteps on the footpath close behind me. I ran until I came to Sister Josephine and Sister Angelica, dropped the magazine on their pile, and kept on running.

The high tower

Nicko is at my shoulder again, water beading on his skin, laughing that I haven't moved.

'I'm going to,' I say. 'In a minute.'

Nicko shakes his head to dry himself, like a happy dog, and a few drops of water fly onto my back. I shiver even though it's thirty degrees and not even midday.

'She's looking, you know,' Nicko says, and slaps his shorts with his hands. It makes a deep, dank sound like a wet towel hitting the floor.

I look over to the grass area by the pool before I think about it, and then pretend I'm not. I swing my eyes to the sky, which is a high, cloudless blue, and I reckon it makes sense why I'd be looking at a sky like that.

'Girls don't care about that stuff any more,' I say, still looking up, my eyes aching from the glare. 'Never did probably.'

But I'm not sure I believe it. If girls didn't care, what was I doing up here? Why had I followed when Nicko said who's coming and led the way to the high tower? What was the point if not girls?

'We used to say only mental cases jumped off here,' I say.

Nicko laughs but doesn't say anything. When we were kids, me and Nicko would point out the high tower from miles away. We loved the way it rose from the flat nothing of our town and seemed to scrape the sky. We would say we could see bodies going off it, even when the tower was tiny on the horizon, but I don't know if we could see this or just imagined it.

Nicko slaps his shorts, doing something like a drum fill that starts on his thighs and moves up his body. He's always been this way, always moving, like he's keeping rhythm to a beat that never ends and only he knows.

He wears more than one pair of shorts. It's usual for him now. He has four or five pairs on, one on top of the other. He does it so he can jump off the high tower all day, and as one pair comes apart from the force of his arse hitting the water over and over, there's another pair underneath. He's like a lizard shedding skin.

There are other boys on the high tower like Nicko. You can tell them because they walk funny. With all the shorts on, they are too padded and soggy around the middle.

I wear just one pair of shorts. They go to my knees and are made up of squares in different colours. Nicko reckons they make me look like I'm wearing a patchwork quilt.

Nicko stops drumming on his body, takes two big steps and leaps into the air. He swings backwards and into a full spin. His arms come in tight across his body, and he hits the water arse first, one leg out straight and the other tucked to his chest. The splash shoots straight up, nearly as high as the tower, and the top drops seem to hang a moment, as if thinking of never coming down. Water is still falling as Nicko comes to the surface and kicks towards the pool's edge.

I don't know when Nicko learnt to do this, or even when he started jumping off the high tower. Last summer, we had been the same. And the summers before that, stretching back to some point neither of us can remember but had seen in photos, our mums in big round sunglasses and floppy hats, swinging us around in the toddler pool.

We still look like each other, me and Nicko. Tanned, thin as pelican shit, sandy hair that shoots up at the front as if reaching for the sun. People often think we're twins. But now it's like Nicko has leapt ahead and is older than me, even though he isn't.

I step again to the edge of the platform and look down. The water below is deep blue and crowded with bodies. Waves slap against each other and run over the sides, turning the white concrete a dark brown. Radio blares from a speaker, and an announcer is talking over the top of 'Eye of the Tiger', the sound rising and falling with shifts in the breeze.

I reach for the rail that runs along the side of the platform, my fingers and toes tingling. I look down at Nicko, who now sits on the edge of the pool, feet dangling in the water. He is with two girls I haven't seen before. One of the girls is wearing a Guns 'N' Roses T-shirt, knotted at the front. She takes Burger Rings from a pack and tosses them at Nicko, who tries to catch them in his mouth. A Burger Ring bounces off his face and into the water, and they all laugh.

Me and Nicko always had Burger Rings when we came to the pool as kids. We'd put them on our fingers, joke they were diamond rings and act all posh. Or we'd see how many Burger Rings we could get on our fingers, and eat them off one by one. We used to wonder why Burger Rings tasted better at the pool than if you bought them at the shops. We called it pool magic. It became something we said a lot for a summer or two because we thought it was funny for some reason. Pool magic. We said it about everything.

*

Nicko is beside me, puffed from climbing the ladder that zigzags to the top. I ask him who the girls are.

'I dunno,' he says, sucking in the air. 'They just started talking to me. They asked about my shorts. Wanted to know what happens when all the pairs are ripped and if my arse is hanging half out.'

I smile and look over to the kiosk. I'm still thinking about Burger Rings. The kiosk is at the other end of the pool from the high tower, across a stretch of concrete that bakes in the sun and is often too hot to stand on. I think of me and Nicko in the kiosk queue as kids, pocket money in our hands, hopping from foot to foot on the hot concrete, looking up at a menu board that is faded all over except where new prices have been stickered over the old.

Nicko is doing repair work on his shorts. A split has opened up in the outer pair, exposing a bright orange pair underneath. A piece of material flaps freely, and he lifts it one way and then the other, as if wondering whether to tie it up or tuck it in somewhere. He yanks and the piece of material comes away in his hand.

I look down at my shorts and wonder how they would go if I jumped. I imagine the coloured squares scattered over the length of the pool as if I've exploded on impact.

Nicko takes two big steps and leaps into the air.

*

I look over to where Hannah is. She is sitting on the lawn that stretches away from the side of the pool. She is with our group of our friends, but off to one side. She has only been at the school a few weeks, and I think still feels on the edge of things, and like she belongs at her old school and old town. She has a book in her hand and sunglasses on, but it's hard to tell if she's reading or where she's looking. The book is *The Bell Jar*, which we're doing in English. I wave, but she doesn't wave back.

'I don't think she can see us,' I say to Nicko. 'She can't see far without her glasses.'

Hannah sits up the front in English so she can see the board better. I sit behind her a few seats. Last week during a class discussion about Sylvia Plath's life, I said Plath was too good for Ted Hughes and that Hughes was a lying, cheating turd. Our teacher, Ms Hooper, said it was good I had expressed an opinion, but that I shouldn't have used a word like turd. But I hardly heard what Ms Hooper was saying, because at that moment Hannah turned around in her seat, held her fist up and mouthed the words 'lying, cheating turd'.

I had played the scene over in my head a few thousand times since then. So many I worried the vision would lose clarity or disappear entirely. But it hadn't yet. I actually thought I saw more now. Such as the way Hannah's dark hair fell over her eyes when she held her fist up, and how the silver bangle she wore had caught the sun from the window and thrown a pocket of light around the room.

I look over now to see if Hannah is wearing the bangle, but it's too far to tell. She is lying on her back, propped on her elbows, her book open on her tummy. She has taken off her sunglasses and is squinting into the sun, a blue cloth hat pulled low on her forehead. Maybe she is looking at me like Nicko said.

*

'I can't do it,' I say.

Nicko is working on his shorts again. He rips a piece off and throws it. The material catches a breeze and takes off. It twirls as if happy, or like it's writing messages in the air. It dips and glides, finds a fresh current and floats up again. It flies towards the kiosk, and over the lawn, high above where Hannah lies on her towel. It comes back over the pool, and drifts down, lazy as an autumn leaf. It lands at the shallow end next to a bald Dad in a rashie.

'I can't do it,' I say again. I tell Nicko to swap shorts with me. I tell him to put on my patchwork quilt shorts, and I'll put on one of his pairs. I say Hannah can't see far without her glasses and from where she is we'll look the same. I say all she'll see is a blur of colour and tan skin. I tell him that with his new shorts on, he should give a wave in Hannah's direction and jump, and while he did so I would duck down the ladder and slip secretly into the pool, where we'd swap shorts again.

I look at Nicko and bite my bottom lip.

'That's a stupid plan,' he says, and agrees to it immediately. He does a drum roll on his shorts as if to set the plan in motion.

We move to the back of the platform, behind about a dozen people who hang out on the high tower for the sun and smokes. Nicko takes off his ripped shorts, and the orange pair underneath. He gives me the orange pair and puts the ripped shorts back on. I have nothing under my patchwork quilt shorts, so I grab a towel from the rail and wrap it around my waist. I slide off my shorts and hold them out to Nicko.

'Hang on,' he says. 'I don't think these are colourful enough for me.'

We keep low on the platform and get into our new shorts.

Nicko pulls the patchwork quilt shorts over the top of his other shorts, which are wet and cause a drag. He inches the new shorts over his hips, doing little jumps on the spot to move them up. He sucks in his stomach as he fastens the press-stud button. 'It'll be fine if I don't breathe,' he says.

My new shorts are loose because they had gone over the top of Nicko's other pairs. I push out my gut, but there's still a gap at the front. I bunch the excess material in my hand and hold it up, like a kid playing dress-ups.

I look over Nicko's shoulder and past the bodies on the high tower. I can just make out Hannah on the grass. She is lying back on her elbows, knees bent, an ankle resting on her other leg.

'Okay, go now,' I say. 'And remember to jump like I would.'

'I'll be sure to jump like a wuss,' Nicko says.

He holds out his arm for a fist bump, but steps away before I get my hand out, and I wave my arm after him in the air as he slips between the smokers and sunbakers towards the edge of the platform.

I put my hand on the curved rail at the top of the ladder, ready to move. I look over the heads to Nicko, then towards Hannah. A voice crackles over the loud speaker saying a boy has lost his mum and is waiting at the lifeguard station. When the radio breaks back in, sounding somehow louder than before, Nicko gives a wave in the direction of the grass area and jumps.

He is not used to jumping this way. He spins his arms forward, but his body wheels backwards, until he's almost horizontal. He stops his arms and becomes very still as if he hopes no movement will help where rapid movement didn't. But this only seems to increase the speed at which he's moving. He windmills his arms in the other direction, as if in a final wish to rewind and start over. Metres from the pool, his arms and legs are kicking in all directions, like someone tangled in a sleeping bag.

He hits the water with a crack that seems to shake the trees. Children look up from their play. There is a moment of terrible silence that is broken only by groans from the high tower.

I lean over the side rail and look down. I can see my patchwork quilt shorts. Nicko is in them, but he is hardly moving. He is floating face down, and the skin on his back is red from where he hit the water.

I race down the ladder, skipping rungs, one hand sliding down the rail, the other holding my shorts up. But before I reach the first landing, I back into a bunch of girls coming up. I climb over the handrail, and try to edge past them. But there's no way down. The girls are tight together, and they keep coming, all of them turning to each other and laughing and making sure everyone behind is still with them and not chickening out.

I bolt back up the ladder, and on the platform I shout for the girls to hurry. But my voice comes out soft and croaky and disappears beneath the song from the speakers.

I turn towards the edge of the platform. The sun is suddenly brighter and I shield my eyes. The bodies around me become like silhouettes and the noise of the pool seems to drop away. An image comes into my head of me and Nicko in the toddler pool, our mums standing over us in big round sunglasses and floppy hats, blocking out a sun that radiates all around them.

And then I am pushing past the bodies on the high tower. And then I am jumping into the air. And then I am falling, and falling, and falling, and the water is rushing towards me. And then I am under water and everything is quiet except the sound of air racing through my body.

*

I come up swinging my arms, pushing to get higher out of the water. My chest aches and my lungs scream. Water slaps into my face, stinging my eyes. I gulp for air, and swallow a mouthful of water. The taste of chlorine burns at the back of my throat.

I spin around, unsure where the side of the pool is. My vision is blurry, a swirl of blues. I rub my eyes and turn around again. And then I see Nicko. His mouth is below the waterline but I can tell he's smiling because his eyes are smiling. His head comes fully out of the water.

'Hey, Davy,' he says, and shakes his head, water flying from his hair in a perfect arc that catches the sun. He puts a hand on his shoulder and grimaces. 'Shit, that hurt.'

We swim to the side of the pool, and rest our arms on the edge, both of us sucking in big breaths. Our legs sway and kick gently in the water.

'Thanks for coming for me,' Nicko says.

I cough and can hear water sloshing around inside me. I shake my head to one side and then the other. My ears clear and suddenly everything sounds loud and tinny. I think of asking Nicko if he did it all on purpose – the jump, the hitting the water, the floating face down. But I don't. And in the silence that follows maybe Nicko guesses what I'm thinking.

'Put it down to pool magic, Davy,' he says.

I look over to Hannah on the grass. She has her sunglasses on. She is reading *The Bell Jar*. The radio is playing 'Our Lips Are Sealed', but she doesn't seem to notice the noise or anything else much around her. She just reads her book.

'Nicko,' I say.

'Yeah,' he says.

'I lost my shorts somewhere.'

We both look down into the water. My skin shimmers beneath the surface, tanned mostly, but in other parts a glowing white.

Nicko cracks up. 'My shorts are still on me, unfortunately,' he says.

The patchwork quilt shorts gleam against the white of the pool wall.

Nicko turns around and faces the middle of the pool. 'I'll find your shorts, Davy,' he says. He pushes off the edge, swims a few strokes, and dives under, his feet kicking a moment at the surface before they disappear.

www.ingramcontent.com/pod-product-compliance
Lightning Source LLC
Chambersburg PA
CBHW051234210726
48290CB00003B/953